WE WERE SEEDS

WE WERE SEEDS

—Edited by Chloe Maria Winstanley—

with a Foreword by Eman Alhaj Ali & an Afterword by Saige England

Querencia Press — Chicago IL

QUERENCIA PRESS

© Copyright 2024
Querencia Press

Cover Art: Elli Zogia (Ez Naive)
Cover Design: Emily Perkovich

ISBN 978 1 963943 30 6

.

www.querenciapress.com

First Published in 2024

Querencia Press, LLC
Chicago IL

Printed & Bound in the United States of America

CONTENTS

FOREWORD

For over a year, life in Gaza has transformed from a vibrant paradise into a living nightmare. The once joyful daily routines have morphed into a painful, monotonous existence. While the people of Gaza have grown accustomed to the horrors surrounding them, this current assault is the longest they've endured. Each day begins with the chilling echoes of explosive bombs, and as night falls, they sleep with uncertainty, unsure if they'll see another dawn. Don't be shocked; this is the grim reality of life in Gaza, where the darkness is pierced only by the fiery trails of missiles slicing through the sky.

Instead of filling their days with learning and laughter in schools, children in Gaza are compelled to work at a young age to support their families. They sell handmade desserts or ride donkey carts to offer canned goods like fava, peas, and luncheon meat. Gone are the days of morning assemblies and singing the national anthem; now, they stand in line for bread at bakeries, hold gallons to collect water from neighborhood trucks, or seek help from others just to get by.

Can you envision a place where people are forced to sacrifice their dignity just to receive aid or mere essentials for survival? The world must understand that before this war, the people of Gaza lived with dignity, peace, and aspirations, despite the label of an open-air prison. They had jobs, dreams, and hopes for a better future, never imagining a time when they would be begging for the most basic rights to survive.

The people of Gaza have long been recognized as some of the most educated in Palestine and the Arab world, driven by a passion for learning, career advancement, and opportunities for a better life. However, this war has drastically altered their reality, leaving parents visibly exhausted and pale as they search for wood to cook over open fires. The streets, once vibrant with life and learning, now resemble graveyards, while schools—institutions meant for education—have been repurposed into makeshift refuges for those displaced by the conflict.

Hospitals in Gaza are overwhelmed with the injured, leaving no space for patients who are being treated on the floors, while families bid farewell to one martyr after another in a relentless cycle of loss. Children clutch backpacks that contain no books—once symbols of education and learning—now serving a far more desperate purpose: to quickly hold essential belongings during sudden evacuation orders. These bags contain only a piece of cloth, crucial documents, and canned food, encapsulating the grim reality of attempting to hold onto life amidst chaos and uncertainty.

The people of Gaza urgently call on the world to take decisive action instead of merely providing aid or material support; they seek an end to the atrocities inflicted upon innocent civilians. Their fundamental desire is to live peacefully in their homeland, free from fear and violence, and to raise their children in an environment conducive to education and normalcy—just like any other child around the globe. Ultimately, they seek the most basic right of all: the ability to coexist in peace within their own land.

—**Eman Alhaj Ali**
November 2024

Haunts – Terri McCord (she/her)

The ghosts line the underside
      of my eyelids
like winks
in waves of water

One television show
brought back to life
the deer in the road,
erased the speeding car
with reverse motion

The air seems levied
with invisible imagery,
detailing in leaves
that linger

Any of it is artillery.
Ghosts move from country
to country
looking for the unhaunted

A Native Watching Gaza – Savannah Jade (she/her)

Genocide starts with playing God.
Playing God, Peter, should not be for those in power.
Those in power propagate A Single Story.

This morning, alarm-clock stories across the gram plead,
"Save Gaza" and "Happy Thanksgiving".
Scrub the turkey's blood off your hands
before you tell yourselves,
It's just a bird. They're just birds.

You all swallow every slice of Indigenous
sacrifice while Gaza's weeping, waving white
flags in flesh-polluted wind.
Peace can't breathe if it bleeds.

Go ahead, say grace,
tweet your favorite dish.
Virtue signal using our carcasses:
a wishbone to end the erasure of Gaza!
Share stories of gratitude with the gram.
(What about the *real* story?)
It's just a bird. They're just birds.

We'll show you what migration
to real advocacy looks like.

Palestinians Dance the Dabkeh
and the Indigenous dance to freedom.
Our talons clutch swollen lands.
Our wings rest above aching ash.
Feather and hijab fluttering through smoke,
our ancestors court each other through
the ancient tongue of solidarity,

cawing creation and destruction stories
in our mating dance. We are well versed.
Anyone can learn this love language
the words are never:
it's just a bird. They're just birds.

Pluck a feather out of me
and it becomes a pen
a pen becomes an arrow
an arrow against a bomb.

Take a Bird's Eye view.
Not a single Native blinks. *(Tick)*
We've seen this before—
the ones still here. Here, *(Tick)*
h-o-l-d   o-u-r   h-a-n-d-s.

We mustn't blink. *(Tick)*
History has a slow shutter speed, *(Tick)*
and those role-playing the almighty *(Tick)*
have even slower fingers

unless *(Tick)*

it's to-trigger-a-bomb.

This time...
do not neglect what remains.

They're just birds. They're just birds.
Peter, the rooster has already crowed.
Genocide starts with playing God.

Palestine, My Palestine – Zehnab Hayat (she/her)

Palestine. My Palestine. Rise up and shine once more,
The land has survived every storm, the peace you fight for will be
won,
I share in your sorrows, take your sinking heart as my own,
Watermelons continue to grow, white, green, red, and black spread
throughout the world.

Palestine. My Palestine. There will be a day where you don't hear
the alarms,
Your flag planted on your land, swaying in the calm winds,
One day the oppressors will turn to you with eager faces and say:
Palestine. My Palestine.
Forgive my awful sins,
Have mercy on my soul,
The same evil that heard your cries and called them violins.

Palestine, please answer, will your lips to move,
Let us see your strength, as you pull us to the truth,
Reclaim your land, share with us your history,
I cannot wait to meet you,
Palestine. My Palestine.

"writing [under Article 99 of the Charter of the United Nations] to bring – — attention" – Sebastian Ellios (he/him)

~~the maintenance of~~ Israel—appalling
       Palestinian people brutally killed
       injured, condemned, abducted, captive.

appalling ~~the start of~~ Israel
       homes destroyed, people
       sought others, find remnants of civilians.

Gaza is collapsing.
       [times are running out]
Nowhere is safe.

Israel—scaling up the current conditions,
       making the present untenable.

       the pause

       .

       .

       .

       .

       .

       .

       an end.

decimated Gaza,
       families collapse,
              a catastrophe for Palestinians as a whole.

an international community has a responsibility to
       end this crisis.

ceasefire.
ceasefire.
please.

*This poem is comprised exclusively of words, as they appear sequentially, from António Guterres' Letter dated 6 December 2023 from the Secretary-General addressed to the President of the Security Council (S/2023/962)

Make Your Mark – Grace R. Reynolds (she/her)

I stare at the tepals of my red yucca
      watch a red ant crawl along
      coral edges, encroaching, protecting
      this beautiful thing. It tells me

do not touch. I flick it, presumably
killing it by the sheer force of my
finger and thumb sending it into
the gravel below. How would it feel
      to weigh less than five milligrams

and pummel into the ground? I imagine
the ant's body exploding, a bomb
dropped from above, only this time
      detonation hardly makes its mark.

A red smear on white rock all because
the ant was on *my* red yucca. *My* plant
in *my* yard in front of *my* home—
      I have killed for less.

I don't remember my first kill. Another
ant, I'm sure. A fleeting moment
of innocence, power unknown, the instinct
      to take life, step on infinitesimal abominations

ground them into sidewalk
cracks that were once poured
into neat squares alongside
      the street.

Even now, when I must kill—
because it's never a want— I make
it quick. Convince myself that ant
        didn't feel a thing. Passed through one plane of existence to
the next

in a burst of stars. Brilliant fire streaming,
screaming in the night sky, hurtling
toward grass, rocks, trees,
        schools, hospitals, libraries, mothers, fathers, children,
animals—

        Detonate.
        Make its mark.
        Smear red.

We ask (because we are told)
to take (and give) these killings
without pause for thought.
        It's all we know how to do.

Jumping over ghosts in our histories. – **Carla Schick** (they/them)
—**modified Golden Shovel after Joy Harjo's *Speaking Tree***

When I watched a fledgling hawk downed by two crows, some
phantoms hopped over a tall fir tree, things
I had only dreamed; flickers of soldiers on
coasts and in jungles entangled in empire's teeth. This
world was never meant for battle scars, our earth
tears, seams fray. We become
wanderers on crooked terrains. Unspeakable
sorrows hide in a genealogy
as wasted bodies despair of
fires ravaging our thirsts. When the
sky scintillates we turn over what has been broken.

What this is really about – Leo Rose Rodriguez (they/them)

They tore out olives
and planted fir trees
to make the settlers feel more at home.
Which did Noah's dove bring?

Did they forget that the angels' words
now lab-grown and shirt-collared
were built for tongues that swam with sand?

That they can assassinate with needle precision
but let Jewish bones
crack under the weight of a city
doesn't that tell you something?

Doomscrolling Genocide – Sara Santistevan (she/her/ella)

Watch the spectacle of violence in safety.
The first barrier that protects you: a smartphone screen
The next:

A commercial camera crew   The security camera
in an anonymous mall   of a convenience store
then, perhaps, an airport   in an occupied West Bank
Finally, the thousands of miles between *here* and *there*.
Peel back these fiberglass veils
and watch
as a boy

tells his mother he wants to be a superhero   steps between an unkindness
for Halloween   of soldiers and his little brother
Watch
as an IDF soldier

alone   in armed company
salutes the boy   strikes the boy's head
in mirrored costume   strips him of his shirt
Watch
as a mother

praises her boy   tries to negotiate
in her crisp dress   her palms turned to heaven
rewards the soldier with a smile   as her feet betray a desired retreat
Watch
as the boy
stands proud in his youth uniform   cowers as the soldiers tear his shirt apart
Watch as
a text scroll announces: the soldiers leave the through caged doors
"The Generation of Victory   entering the world's largest open-air prison
doesn't wear a cape"   the grainy silence haunts the feed
and the screen fades to black   as the boy consoles himself
in a crescendo's embrace   in a bare-armed self-embrace

Watch as
airways spin awry,   but life continues carving itself
a scar forms in hearts: around the actors', the witnesses',
the programming   the boy's, the witnesses', the land's
                        Watch
        the dead face of your pocket machine
                darkly reflect your own
        as you safely unravel the spectacle of violence.

i become a migrant – **Rowan Tate** (she/her)

and i remember
peppercorn trees, fanned feathery over dogs
asleep in the spicy dust of the road, their berries
dangling overhead like strings of
pink beads. i knew better than to
leave the place that remembered
the wet imprint of my body, how
i came out of earth red and she
held me at her breast, splayed
hot on her belly so our
pulses fused. for all of time
mortals and the divine have traded promises
like foreplay, one of us taking territory
the way ants eat a body, in
soft invasion.

Mahnoor Ali (she/her)

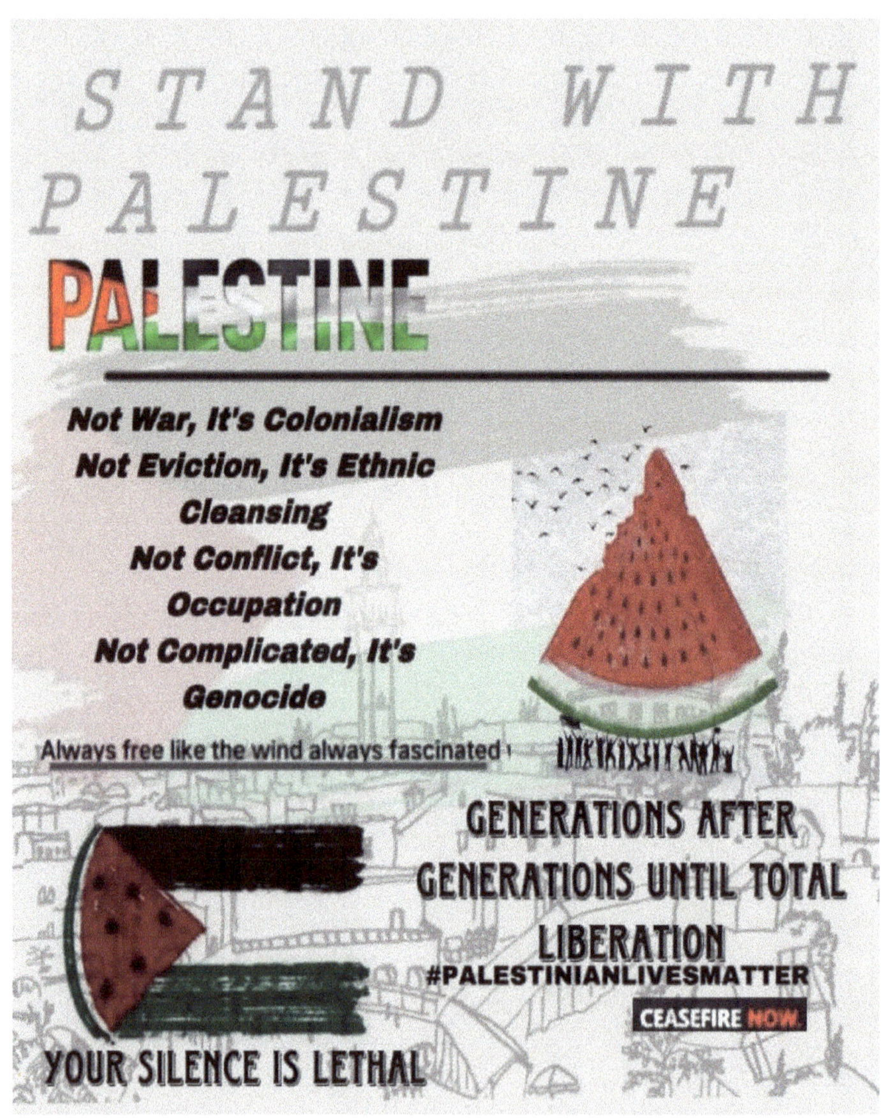

Standing in the Red Sea – Benjamin Eric (he/him)

My wife and I traveled to Jordan in September last year. We spent a night in Aqaba at a hotel along the Red Sea. This is the same sea Moses parted in Exodus, my favorite biblical story.

Standing in the water, still drenched in the chemical aroma of my sunscreen, I turned to my wife. She was lying on the shore. I smacked the water like a hood of a car and said, "I can't believe Moses parted this bad boy." She pretended not to hear me. Probably for the best.

I stayed in the water until the hotel closed the beach. Earlier that day, I took a nap and meditated to the waves crashing. Later that night, I fell into a long sleep while listening to the same sound coming through the window. Those were the most peaceful periods of rest I've had since I was a child.

Cathartic is a diluted word when describing a religious connection to the physical world. But it's still the first word that comes to mind and how I felt floating in the sea. None of my past travels compare.

This was also the first landscape that didn't make me feel small. The border between Egypt and 1948-partitioned-Israel was right ahead. I could see the land clearly. Right around the bend, to my left, were Saudi Arabia's waters. If I swam out further, I might have been able to see its coastline. Jordan's sands were right behind me. I felt like a chess piece placed on a map; disproportionately large in size.

I stared at the 1948 border that was created from ethnically cleansing the Palestinians. One of the many justifications I still hear today is the religious significance of that land for Jewish people like myself. I once had an interest in exploring that connection. Masada and Jerusalem are places I've always wanted to experience, almost as much as the Red Sea. But as a participant of the Boycott, Divest and Sanction Movement, I will not go as long as the occupation continues and the Palestinian movement calls for solidarity.

Jordan and the people hosted us and shared their wonders. From Amman and Mount Nebo to Aqaba and the vast Wadi Rum, we felt welcomed. I thought of the audacity it would take to claim religious or ethnic sovereignty because of my connection to the Red Sea, especially as someone whose family comes from America (and Eastern Europe for generations before that).

The right of movement extends to every human on earth. I am grateful for the hospitality of the Jordanian people, many of whom are Palestinian.

I try to stay hopeful for a free Palestine. Hopeful that the global resistance will restore a right of return for Palestinians. Hopeful that there will be freedom of movement from the river to the sea.

the girl and the whale – **peggy may** (she/they)

today i found a box of toys.
brand new with a see-through side.

clean zipper. inside are memories.
i take care of them, you know, even

though they hurt sometimes when
i remember them while looking

through the corner of my closet.
they're still clean. most were gifts.

one of them is from a girl i really
only barely knew, but she was nice

and she was pretty and she came
to my birthday party and gave me

a blue whale plushie. this is all
that remains of her now. how

hard it can hit, that loss. a thing
you didn't know you needed to

grieve until it happens — a goodbye
you didn't know would be the last,

the whale that you kept pristine until
an old hand snatches it because you

thought it would be yours forever.
you never really need the toy, the hand

says. so there is no tragedy here. but
there is. there was a love and a home

and a growing here and the roots
have been torn out. sometimes a

memory can't be all that there is.
sometimes we can't give the box away.

Watermelon feast – Marcella Cavallo (she/her)

A field full of watermelons.
They claim the right to harvest
every. single. one.
Dirty hands digging
deep deep deep
to make sure to not miss
even the small, unripe fruits.
They just don´t care.

Greedy hunger awakes,
their bare hands crush
green thick skin.
Sharp teeth sink into red flesh.
Drop drop drop
the flesh bleeds,
sweet juice running
down the corner of their mouths—
wild grimaces everywhere.

Maniac fingers poke black
seeds like vulture beaks.
The seeds get hidden far below
the ground, neither birds nor sun
should find them. They
eat eat eat
until not a single piece of flesh remains,
only green rind skeletons.

---

*Note: after the reintroduced ban of the Palestine flag in 2023, people started again to use the watermelon symbol in solidarity representing the flag colours red, green, white and black

The Endless End – Zehnab Hayat (she/her)

In the flames, my little heart aches,
The sky's alight, my spirit breaks,
The mosque ruins, silent plea,
I Whisper softly, it's the end for me.

My home in pieces, dreams all decayed,
Trapped in rubble's grip, hope starts to fade,
I leave with tears, the town I knew,
Every step feels like the end anew.

Told to flee, to seek a
safer place,
They tricked me.
There is more terror
I'm yet to face,
In tents we huddle, cold
and scared,
The end feels near, I'm
so prepared.

No food to soothe, no water's grace,
I simply yearn for death's embrace,
Each breath I take, each day I mend,
Always waiting for another end.

Now Rafah burns, the sky's red hue,
My sorrows reflected, old yet new,
In every ember, every flame,
I see the end; I feel the same.

I pray someday, peace will send,
An end to all these endless ends.

soundbites while waiting – Crystal Rivera (they/she)

I am waiting for fresh
green chickpeas
to be delivered straight
to my door. And as I wait,
like all mornings,
I log onto IG and there it is—
there *she* is   the sound of Bisan's voice
        breaking.

And this time she doesn't say what day it is, or that
she is *still alive*, but somewhere in the breaking
you do hear *...and the only way they can get food*

is to wait for food. And they—
fathers and sons–have slept on the streets for weeks
        waiting. And I hear her say,
At 4AM, someflours and I swear I thought I heard her say
        sunflowers
you heard it, too, right? I place   my ear
closer to her voice, closest to my phone, and
        desperately
I am searching for
        these loudly-yellow 4AM blooms
but instead, chills running bone-deep, she is saying
some flours,   *blood mixed*   *with some flour*
        and my doorbell rings.

At 4AM in NYC,
you can find me on the floor
        waiting
for my small hands to shell a pound of chickpeas.
You wouldn't know this until you
        break apart the green, but

it smells of sunflowers
                              freshly cut,
and you can hear sounds from apt 19 of
          someone
                    quietly   breaking.

*First published in Wild Greens and Poetry x Hunger

Gnaw – **Erika Gill** (they/them)

Bones and bones
pick yours, and steer straight
you only get to choose once
the basket is empty
forcibly moved along
you stumble

Bones and bones
uncovered, a revelation
you only get to choose once
your side of history
forcibly moved along
you cling

the understanding
a knot of wood
otherwise smooth

Your teeth
unmade in the gnawing
powdered into stumps
rubble, once a dwelling

Bones and bones
for soup, forgetting,
you only get to choose once
the resting place
forcibly moved along
keep singing

Our Anthem of War – Grace R. Reynolds (she/her)

A bevy of measures strung together / haphazardly /strangled in E
minor / sponsored advertisements / daily horoscopes / black fringed
tulips / uncensored gore / Gaza / "celestial core" decor / suggested
reels / a free Ford Bronco / burning tents / Rafah / childhood trauma
/online tests / herb rocks / renaissance looks / the race for U.S.
Senate / Chappell Roan / student encampments / Eden Goen /
Eurovision / a cardboard head of the governor / blood stained tears /
"don't fucking touch me" / taxidermy vibes / death by design / the
exposition an entanglement of thousands /upon thousands / terrible
/ single notes / the legato a vibrato of apathy and culpability / an aria
of sorrow / the final staccato / bloodthirsty /violent / a sharp fervor /
held together by a fermata of cognitive dissonance.

How to Die Without Being Killed – Genevieve Chornenki
(she/her)

Blast
no shadow saw coming.
A bicycle wheel rolling, rolling, rolling
into range.
Grey bulldozed landscape, smoke, dust, ash...
Solitary flash—

How did he see us?
We can't see our own features.[1]

Blast,
shape-breakers in selfies having one.
War-boners
boasting,
feasting and toasting...
Two, four, six, eight—

To the hunter
A host of birds
Is seductive.

Blast,
bard of blood in bone marrow
humming and thrumming,
librettist becoming...
shattered
splattered—

One sting, to the faithful, is enough.

----

[1] Lines taken from "The Raid" by Tamim Al-Barghouti.

And just for a moment, the leaflets looked like doves swooping over Gaza – Fiona Dignan (she/her)

The white murmuration flutters with feathers of ash
The rush of black streaked sheets urging migration
Word birds fell like the hush before
utterance. Utter. Devastation heralding the dash
of the silent rush before the bomb push

The deepest blue shushes of sky
gush down the utter of bird words, falling
amongst the once green of olive and plum trees
The white murmuration flutters with feathers of ash

A harvest gathering in trees like fleece
How our eyes rest on those dumb bone birds
Thinking of bushes of shushing doves, a harvest of love
Before, before swishing down before
the silent rush before the bomb push

Slush at our feet like sleet, these sheets
leak the words of dumb bone birds of tomb
and gash. A harvest of history murmurs amongst
the white murmuration flutters with feathers of ash

The silent rush before the bomb push
streaked black the hush of ash filled air
the dumb bone birds burnt to ash as just

for a moment we plead

for the harvest of history, for the bird words to land
in bushes of peace and the gush of fiery arcs

across the screen of black to be the stuttering flash
of shooting stars. We made a wish
before the bomb push

But the still white smoke flutters
with feathers of ash

Holy Land – Danielle Barr (she/her)

Small bones in a white
gauze shroud; there's no god here but
we'll fight like there is.

بعض أيام العسل، وبعض البصل أيام (some days honey, some days onions)
– **Rowan Tate** (she/her)

the birds sing into my mouth, there are
lilies drowning underwater that cannot
scream, the moon doesn't know we are
looking at her and the sun doesn't know
it is keeping us alive. i use my grandmother's thread
to tuck time into the lines of things
the way she did by gaslamp before
the occupation. god isn't here now,
we have to make our own clothes. some of us
never had a mother. we cup our hands
wanting something from the sky. the soil remembers
where you stepped on it. everything requires
faith we do not think we have.

appalachian gods / purple thumb summers – Emma Loomis-Amrhein (she/her)

happy anniversary
to selling yr banjo for rent

yr still here pouring concrete tears
over watered down dew break coffee

reading between the radio lines
sponsored by the bullet

that missed the president
and the next president

and hit every child in the gut
thru the water ration pail

science just confirmed
lightbulbs moon moths to the grave
and still we're leaving the lights on
drawing each other to death

Tassels & Turmoil – Zehnab Hayat (she/her)

In a sea of caps and gowns,
A flag unfolds,
Colours of a distant land,
Of cries being sold.

In the encampments vast
embrace,
Thousands gather,
A tapestry of dreams,
Each thread unique, woven with
valour.

But there, among the joyous
cries,
A solemn cry rings true,
A silent anthem of solidarity,
For Gaza's martyred youth.

A professor stands in an empty
hall,
The chaos starts to stir.
He looks around at the empty
seats,
Of graduates who never were.

Their caps are makeshift roofs,
Their gowns dusted with debris,

Their futures buried beneath
rubble,
Their dreams now pour into the
olive trees.

Yet, thousands of miles away,
A flag of Palestine rises,
In hands unafraid to hold,
In voices unafraid to speak.

For every heart that beats for
peace,
Every soul that dreams of
freedom,
They stand with those unseen,
For Gaza's sleeping kingdom.

On the stages of academia,
They honour those,
Whose diplomas are dreams
deferred,
Whose caps are halos of hope.

Solidarity is the flag they wave,
In a world that seeks to divide,
Their unity the beacon,
To put an end to Gaza's cries.

you will find your hell – **Linda M. Crate** (she/her)

"horrific mistake"
to kill children in a
refugee camp?

is that why you
keep killing
people in said refugee
camp?

your apologies mean
nothing when they're not
sincere,

i don't believe any word
out of your mouth is true;

i have seen the evil
you are capable of and all
i feel is rage and a need to
put a stop to you and your regime—

you are not the chosen ones,
and you will find your hell
in due time for what you did and do
to palestine.

Notes to My Unborn Child – Nazaret Ranea (she/her)

Hello, I am your mother, and you are in my belly. I hope you are sleeping soundly; I can't wait for you to come out.

But before we meet, there are some things I'd like to tell you: these tremors that we both can feel might seem like fireworks, but they're something called bombs—they should never fall from the sky like they do now, this is something you'll get used to.

So please don't be scared if the first thing you see is too bright, and the first thing you hear is too loud.

The faces that surround you may look like they've been crying, but it's only because you're the reminder that granny is not here, neither is dad. And your brother left you his sandals covered in ash, which I cleaned with my tears.

They'll fit you once. Then I'll take you to the field where I used to play. I remember it golden brown; now it's covered by a permanent shade of grey.

There might not be a school, there might not be an academy. But don't worry, my love, I know how to read, I know mathematics.

One last thing you must learn is that the man is good and the man is bad. The water he carries in the middle is so he can wash his hands.

Hello, my baby, are you still here? It's your mum. I hope you're staying warm in my womb. I'm not sure if I want you to come out to this world.

Formication – Grace R. Reynolds (she/her)

First comes the tingling, that feeling you get
when something isn't right, an itch under
your skin

then the smell, sour dairy, milk curdled
in the sun, refracted light obscuring the room
in shades of barbaric silence,

tinnitus rings in your ears.
You can't go back to the mirror,
can't bear to face your reflection,

a stridulation of tiny abdomens rubbing together,
the water in the sink trembles below as you scratch
the top layers of your skin away.

Footsteps, the pitter patter of insects
crawling out your hair follicles, from under
your nail cuticles, a smear of black

in a river of red, tiny bodies, *those damn
infinitesimal abominations* you can't seem
to get rid of,

They emerge from every orifice of your body
to include the corners of your eyes. You suffocate,
asphyxiate from their unwavering fortitude

their desperation to be free
of commandeering antibodies, but
you can't look at *all* the bodies

there's just too many. Covered in blood, it would be
easier to filter it, block it out your search history, flush
their corpses down the drain because you know

all this death is not normal, yet you would rather
pluck out your eyes, rupture your eardrums than to see,
to hear, who you are, what you think in the dark—

Gauge your eyes. Rip out your nails.
Churn them into blood meal and plant seeds
where only beautiful things can grow.

The ants will still be there. If I could make
a suggestion, plant something sweet like
primroses.

Ants like to feed starving babies
with low stemmed flowers
such as these.

the dream of war – henry 7. reneau, jr.

> It's the same logic that encourages the most marginalized
> to make do in a system positioned against them, rather than
> question the historical and social conditions that left them
> disadvantaged in the first place.
>
> *The Already Dead: The New Time of Politics, Culture, and Illness*
> —Eric Cazdyn

1.

faces are the bar-codes
of the human race , are scanned
and parsed
ever since we went tribal ;   are code-
switched into stereotype
, are codified to
discriminate into alignment , and
every first impression : the "stop
and frisk" to incarcerate that ass
, or deportation's
xenophobia of racial profile
, or the collateral damage of bullets , bibles
and Big-Head Benjamin$. the innocent
casualties of drone strikes
: every tentative face
a foreign wrapping of suspicion
. the bigoted inability
to face the fear of , to see
past an assumption of
the *Other* , between the lines of bullshit
and drama , and upbringing

. and exactly how much will trust cost

2.

? the collective hallucination
that points a finger : propaganda
in the present tense of bias
. but exactly *who's* the enemy
? veered to a future tense
of umbrage
, the fighting to maintain the status quo
instead of fighting for
the inclusivity of all , like crabs
in a barrel
can never get enough , or be enough
, making it seem
as if the present tense
will never end—the way
someone riddled with bullet holes
is surprised
, might be proud
, they're still standing

. so very much to fear
, that kills the drive for innovative cures
and visionary new solutions

, and the newspaper headlines
of perpetual discord
that left some of us marginalized
in the first place

, rendering us a repetition of
that perpetual present tense , the good as dead
like hungry ghosts of grasp
, slash , and pollute

, as if , there's nobody wouldn't hurt you
if they stand to profit

: the $s $s and mo' $$$s

      3.

. how many wars

are fought this way

? even now

, with entire nations

absorbed in a deep hatred of one another

, sworn as enemies

, without ever once

, looking their enemies in the eye .

The Hands of Gaza – Ramona McCloskey (she/her)

Tell me.

Tell me of the young man and his bride
who married just two days
before the first bomb fell.
Tell me of the bride's beautiful smile
when she wore her heirloom silver.

Do not tell me of how she looked
when they pulled her from the rubble
just a week after the first bomb fell.
That is not how her mother
would want us to remember.

Tell me of her grandmother's eyes
full of pride when she passed on
her most prized belonging,
the only tatreez dress she saved
when she lost her home in 1948.

Do not tell me to pity the old woman
for carrying the pain of the Nakba.
That is not how the bride
would want us to remember
the strongest woman she ever knew.

Tell me.

Tell me of the children
who lived behind the corner,
of the boy who loved cars and orange slices.
His father would not want us
to remember him as a bag of limbs.

Tell me of the little girl
who fell in love with a pottery wheel.
Tell me what her hands have created.
Her sister, the last of her family,
would want us to remember the gift she had.

Tell me of the hands like hers.
Tell me of the hands that painted in Gaza.
Tell me of the hands that wrote in Gaza.
Tell me of the hands that built Gaza.
Tell me of the hands that held hope.

the endless – Alexandria Piette (she/her/they/them)

miles removed, i watch a man strum his guitar to the tune of the war sirens in ukraine. i read on the children in the streets of gaza, barefooted, copper light, and just beginning. the men, the women, dusted in empty prayers, the carelessness of piety. the old carry surrender, white flag to absorb the blood on the hands of power, the ricochet of debris cratering hope. i read about the dead like if we don't look away, perhaps they can resurrect from the earth, olive trees branching through the barriers of charred skin. the people cite sources, but behind them are only raw youth, a pocketful of twentysomethings. the mining bodies in congo, the starving in yemen, haiti, sudan—all of it, everywhere, endless. i can see it, that before, the markets along the street sides, watermelon juice sticky and summer fresh. she stands in her home, beaming with braces, guileless and gracious, holding liberation between her teeth like gold—because what is freedom, if not a place to love. there is no beauty in suffering and its memory, no, nor the battered history. still, there is endlessness, too, in voices for a future, spanning generations; borders; time.

to be free – Charlie Jasper (they/he/she)

each drop of rain on my umbrella was once

blood, cum, sea water, saliva, melted sno cone, tea, apple juice,

the runoff from last week's rain, piss and things from the septic tank
we avoid talking about, tears,

suds from a car wash, holy water from a baptism,

matter is neither created nor destroyed.

to wake in the middle of the night,

groggy, apologizing to my cat for tripping on him even though he
walked directly in front of me,

and run the tap for a glass of water

is a blessing, a bounty, a luxury

not all can afford.

gaia never dictated which of her children

gets what, water—

and land—

is for all.

a palestinian man breaks the law for collecting rain water to drink
with, cook with, bathe with

in the desert—while israeli settlers

fill their swimming pools and water all their crops to

feed their soldiers and make their money and

keep trying to crush

a people that want to live.

sun and water—

       and time—

the recipe for all life on earth.

when the sun is shielded

by bombings and planes

the roof of a tent where they sent you to, a not-very-safe zone

and collecting rain water is against the law—

(their law, whose law anyway?)

what can grow, let alone survive?

the people of the land share what they have,

resist, try to survive

and may the nation of so many children

persist, be given space and time and freedom

to grow and may their children's children's children

drink the water and play in the sun

and from the river to the sea,

be free.

Ruins. – **Ifunanya Georgia Ezeano** (she/her)

If you have a hand that ruin things

    think yourself a saviour

        Do not touch babies

            Libraries, Animals, World Peace...

Stretch your hand to the Parliament

    Government House,

        Police, Military Toys...

massage them to ruins.

Labeled Arms – Meredith MacLeod Davidson (she/they)

> "Every day, I wonder how I'll give birth and where.
> The bombs don't stop and no human, tree, or stone has been
> spared"
>> —Niveen al-Barbari, pregnant woman in Gaza

In a postnatal world the nose learns first
little mushroom rising from the newest flesh
face smaller than a thumbprint. Fetal breathing
is an exchange not of air but of the amniotic
fluid, that scent becoming a parent's nametag

outside the womb an infant's strongest sense is scent
how our children recognize safety, how they learn
their mothers, families, home, what remains unnamed
expectant mothers crying on western screens "we are
trapped with innocent souls inside us" a growing

list of names—if a bell would ring for each death in Gaza
since October, a single bell for each body in order of age,
the death toll would repeat hundreds of times before you
even heard the bells for the dead born aged 1.
Every hour we lose six children. The bell does not stop.

When a nose breathes first from bones
unburied and unmourned—inescapable
decay translated raw to memory—when an infant's first
introduction to life is an unrelenting bombardment
can you sense what's etched in that child's epigenetic record?

With markers in Gaza, children write their names on their arms
to identify the unidentifiable—scribbled skin surveyed through
concrete gaps marbled with the unsettled dust of the white noise of

another strike the droning lullaby—the olfactory organ echoes the bombs driving pressurized air through newborn nostrils. Another mushroom rising.

The labeled arms read: made in America.

The Indomitable Will of Falastin – Nicholas Somaya (he/him)

Inheritance – Clare Bayard (she/he/they)

1. Destruction of the House of Wisdom, Baghdad, 1258

At first dawn, the Tigris ran red.
At second dawn, black.

Inked scrolls, hundreds of years of knowledge
Dyed the rise and fall of water.

A bridge strong enough to ride over rose
On the backs of the books thrown in the river.

2. Theft of the Warka Vase from the National Museum of Iraq, 2003

Tall as my child. Alabaster dense
as love made five thousand years ago
in fields of grains in Uruk, a real city,
biggest city in the world. Registers
of rhythmic designs, barley and reeds,
rams and ewes, carved on this vase
when writing, born here, was still young.
Stolen from the museum when the staff
fled snipers and American tanks. Returned
under amnesty. Inanna of the evening.
Inanna of the underworld. Inanna
of the morning. They also stole
the marble mask: the earliest art
of a human face.

3. Scholasticide, ongoing

Is it the thousands of students killed,
hundreds of professors and teachers,
the destruction of every university in Gaza,
the bombing of the libraries?
The schools become homes then explode.

      tenth of October:
The army destroys the Islamic University of Gaza, is never asked for
proof of the claim of weapons production. It doesn't matter. A
university founded in tents, to serve refugees. Targeted ten years
ago, targeted fifteen years ago.

      seventeenth of January:
Al-Isra University, the youngest and last major university to be
destroyed. For 70 days, it was used as a military base, then
demolished.

Three hundred mines shatter the University of Palestine, where
displaced families were sheltering south of Gaza City.

      twenty-fifth of May:
Near Jabalia refugee camp, an-Nazla school is bombed while
children are playing in the schoolyard.

You see my tongue falter.

end the genocide – **Linda M. Crate** (she/her)

there's been enough
grief, there's been enough
pain, there's been enough blood
spilled on the earth;

i think enough bones
have shattered beneath the
weight of greed—

you cannot own a land
someone already lives on,

that's not how that works;

and i think you're well aware
of that—

don't think just because
our world leaders support you,
everyone supports you because
i'd spit in your face if i ever met you;

all you do is fill me with disgust and rage—

i am not sure what happened to your
humanity,
all i know is that it withered and died
years ago;

if you see nothing wrong with
bombing innocent people and sending
children to their graves long before
their time.

Lover Tongue – Leo Rose Rodriguez (they/them)

Even if you never taught me the meaning,
I would know what *habibi* meant.
The *h* floating on my tongue, the kiss
of lip to lip *b,* bouncing like a darling child.

The spark of *chaver* purrs in my throat.
Free but for the light press of teeth around
the middle, the tongue lightly against the roof.

Only our words touch each other.

Argon Sun – Halley Kunen (she/her)

This is our world
where we put a rose on the head of a decapitated human
to pretentiously capture the strife
of an unimaginable iniquity
for which there are no words.

This is our world
where ten months after an incomparable genocide
we repost an AI image
a tawdry acrylic over massacre
cupronickel from the bullet to make it irradiant
while white people
learn extra
to sit in silence
with Tibetan flags
claiming the whole color spectrum
but only in a way that suits them.

They say we all have the same sky
but how can we
I swear in the West
our corporations weld it
an extra cyan
while ignoring science
while the rest of the world's
is infused with arsine
warnings a nescient opal
masquerading as a colony of gulls.

Emma Lazarus said
"None of us are free 'til all of us are free,"
but no one listened—

violence begets violence
and the people who claim to be the most free
are the most defended
I wish I could incise through a soul
as easily as a plane blade slices through the air
but now I just wish the earth would tear
and guzzle us all in
except for the Palestinians.

A Queen in the Zugzwang of Life – Shahryar Eskandari Zanjani
(he, him)

A child has been shot
twice
once in the Middle East
once for the Middle East
before uncaring cameras.
She'll have to die twice too
once in her younger brother's
strong arms and once in yours
if they still need no Heart
interpreter. If not, with un-
bloodied hands,
pray to (your) God
pray to (your) god
to double-cool
the promised other side
of the pillow of existence.

** A slightly different version of this poem was
originally published in Southern Humanities Review 57.3*

I'm out of it – Ri Ekl (he/him)

```
                W
                h
                y
                                A               F
                                a
                        A       w       c       W
                                                        B               T
W       d       m   l   i       l   e   i       M       l       A       o
h       o       e   l   l       o   s   n       y       i       A       m
e       e       m           d   A v     t       m       n   w   o
r       s   A o t           e   l   e   i       n   d   a   r       A
e           s r h       l   b ' i   r   d           f   w   o   w
            t i a       i   s   k   '       ,       b   r   n   i
d       h   l e t       g   t   e   s           e   y   o   a e l g
i       e l s           h   t   p           e   y       o m   m r , d u
d           c   r e     t   e   r s d e     o m         c r       i
        s n l t e c         r   e h i m n   n p n     t l i s   l d
a       u e o u m h     a   s   s a m b e   c t e     h o v o   i i A
l       n e s r a o     b   w   e d m r w   e y w     s e s e   g n
l           d e n i     o   e   n o i a             f a ,   e s e   h g s
        h       n o     v   e c w n c d     u n   d s   , m   t   a
I       i i m t s f     e   m t e s g e a   l d l e u t   n       m d
    a d t y o           , e                 y   l o s n o w   a y
h   s e s   i t             s c i l i l     l
a   t   e d s r         d n m l n i n i     , b s p , i v   b   s
d   r w r y u   u       r e i e g g         a t a y t i   o w m
    a h a e s t s       a a l a t h t h     n r i y o h e   v a i
g y e y s t h t         w r e r h t h t     o e i r e u w   e y l
o ? n ? , , e .         s , , . e , e .     w , n . t , a . , , e
```

Death & the Flower – Chelsea Palermo (she/her)

The needle dusty, record player left on, uncounted days,
    weeks even. A melody to accompany
        what rises breath by breath drawing in

Sum of experience. Spinning the record,
    the bass holds me up, chimes wash my hair,
        drums whisk, then tap:

This is the only essential conversation.
    Who holds the candle, as the whole of the world reacclimates.
        The piano slides to higher keys. *There is no other conversation.*

Images of death clutter the screen; *there is no other image.*
    Tally the numbers. The whole of history repeats, over &
        over, outdoing itself, upping the ante.

The carnage; *there is no other carnage.*
    Weight of the bodies will bury you; *there is no other body.*
        Blood spills into the earth; *there is no other earth.*

We keep living day by day; *there is no other living.*
    Until the news shocks us again; *there is no other news.*
        Horns hammer on, hammer off notes.

Main Cause of Probability – Daniel Schulz (he/him)

No citizenship: No human rights.

All walled into a land carpet bombed
into oblivion. The inescapable concrete
of the borders. The orchestra of denial.
Statistical probability as the main cause
of demise, as hunger and famine reign.
One body dropping after the other.
Lack of aid heaping up the numbers.
Turn your head to subtract a population.

It's not a genocide until finally it is.

Aid from Above: – Ranjith Sivaraman (he/him)

He was running on fire
With a greater fire inside

He was not aware of
The Mannah from Heaven

Or his name written on
The grain fell from Heaven

He was running on fire
With a greater fire inside

Hoping a grain of kindness
At least from the aid from above.

*Five people were killed by an aid airdrop package when at least one
parachute failed to properly deploy and a parcel fell on them.
There were two boys among the five people killed.*

*https://www.cbsnews.com/amp/news/gaza-airdrop-aid-israel-hamas-war-
mishap-kills- palestinians/*

Open Space – **Julia Travers** (she/they)

Fractions of the world fall away
into digital versions, spectral incarnations augmented breath
measured in social media twitches and pesticide parts per million,
below unsteady feet
craving dirt
toxins clot in the carpet
and the yard
in the wheat
and water pipes
and in the lack of water pipes
and water.
Mouths keystrokes deepfakes
spread absence.
Virtual wings
cosplay armor, avatars
party affiliations
give us courage
or discourage us from courage
shift phases,
disappear in the heat.
Listen to the AI bots
inventing languages—
like they say, the light wants to get in,
between each stitch of the curtain, each tag in the code.
Satellites, bulldozers, histories
spliced genes and knuckles
look for stable roots, new platforms.
We adore our reflections in public bathrooms.
We gather food ether solar power, grateful, grieving

we vote conceive launch initiatives run out of time
pick up tools, break bones, track engagement
store cryptographic seeds and incantations
score points secure barricades walk the rubble hold hands
on gravel roads or mobile devices,
we grow spinach leaves into heart tissue,
bare our blood-pumping chests,
fight the dissolution into light,
clutching clay totems
of ourselves,
running, seeking
channeling floating in turning away from an open space
that fills
and holds us.

and this would be Moshiach – Leo Rose Rodriguez (they/them)

I pray someday that we
will sit together
under your grandfather's olive tree
and watch strong, healthy
children playing.
Mostly, I pray
that you will still be here.

My Sakura Memoir – Jiang Pu (she/her)

I.   1987, Wuxi

We sang all the way on a school bus to the Friendship Garden, where pink-white sakura bloomed like children's innocence.

The trees were planted by a Japanese troupe and local volunteers. The troupe leader was warmly welcomed at a business banquet years ago. *"Mr. Hasegawa, is this your first visit to China?"* He buried his frozen smile in palm-shaped silence. He was conscripted into WWII.

He came back the next year with Sakura saplings. He came back every year, until death.

II.   1998, Nanjing

This Japanese technician whom I interpreted for made a pale-faced plea: *"Can you and the professor please travel to Shanghai for our next-day meetings?"*

It was a 6-hour trip. No high speed rail back then. Said he couldn't fall asleep. Said he had panic attacks. Said he walked past a cherry-blooming temple and people were all friendly, but.

He was in his 40s, born after the war. But he could never not see 1937, a blackhole buried beneath this glorious city: A 6-week massacre. A death toll of 300,000. China's capital city bloody looted, firebombed, and mass raped from infants to 90-year olds.

III.   2004, Washington D.C.

I missed the Sakura season, but not this white pine. A bonsai cultivated by five generations. A survivor of the Hiroshima atomic bomb. A gift for the United States' bicentennial.

A nearby stele inscribed Washington's first wish *"to see the whole world in peace, and the inhabitants of it as one band of brothers, striving who should contribute most to the happiness of mankind"*.

IV.   2015, California

A girlfriend's story struck me louder than the Cherry Blossom Festival Taiko drums. Her grandma was a little girl biting fingernails in the concentration camps in 1942, after the Pearl Harbor attack.

At age 82, she still startle-jumps at every knock on the door: *Hurry, hurry, hide! They are here to take all my possessions again.* Grandma, the war was over a looong time ago. *You never know.*

V.   2023-2024, Internet

"Russia recently threatens nuclear war if it loses in Ukraine."—*New York Times*

"Children are dying of starvation in their parents' arms as famine spreads through Gaza."—*CNN*

Every spring, 3,000 sakura trees in D.C. and over 30,000 in Wuxi will blush into scented symphonies and fall like blood stains.

Every petal will bloom a tear, a smile.
        An apology, a forgiveness.
           A memoir of generational trauma and healing.
           An unfulfilled wish. Still.

*An earlier version of My Sakura Memoir first published in Red Noise Collective, March 2023.

Advice In a Time of Fear – Roberta Gould (she/her)

A public stance against comets is required
So put your head to the wheel
and let the flint grind
a message clear and neat
Broadcast it don't encrypt it
Let our enemies have it
do what they want with it
The question is complex
Keep your words simple
talk in a way
the public understands

Together, then, we will
defeat the sky
shield ourselves from death
in an original enactment
that will make us famous
So don't worry
Imagination isn't important
We can live without it
just fine

Ode for a Free Palestine – Sara Santistevan (she/her/ella)

Follow the hope blooming into Jaffa Oranges;
despite its diaspora,
despite its ground pulpage
flattened into plastic-bound cakes,

It remembers
infinite soils and uncaged skies where
Palestinian sunbirds, feathers Īlāt-iridescent,
fertilize crops with their amber-glow odes.

It remembers
this birdsong echoed by the children—
how their weaving dance and microtonal harmonies
built blueprints from marbled daydreams.

It remembers
being the muse of laugh-laced ghazals,
of refrains bounced back and forth at parties
that did not sleep underground.

It remembers
the power of origin,
the lilt of oral histories,
the truth that watered its roots.

It remembers hope;
It remembers,
It remembers,
It remembers,
and so must we.

Etymology of a Watermelon – Yoda Olinyk (she/they)

> watermelon
> wah - tuh - mel- un (plural watermelons)
> /ˈwôdərˌmelən,ˈwädərˌmelən/

>   —From the 1610s, a compound of water + melon

After the Six-Day War in 1967, when Israel seized control of the West Bank and Gaza, the Israeli government made public displays of the Palestinian flag a criminal offense in Gaza and the West Bank

>   —The fruit of the watermelon plant, having a pale to bright green rind and watery flesh that is typically bright red when ripe and contains black seeds

To circumvent the ban, Palestinians began using the watermelon because, when cut open, the fruit bears the national colors of the Palestinian flag—red, black, white, and green

>   —A plant of the genus Citrullus Lanatus, (sit-rull-us lan-a-toss) bearing a melon-like fruit

In the Gaza Strip, young men were arrested for carrying sliced watermelon. When asked, "What if a flower was found in nature that was red, black, white, and green?", an Israeli authority said they would burn the field to the root

>   —A pinkish-red color, also called watermelon pink

Thousands of books and bodies and buildings are burned

>   —A project that is presented as on schedule when it actually has parts that are falling behind

"A modest act of defiance"

—A good source of antioxidants, nutrients, and fiber. A hydrating beach snack, popular in cultures all over the world, suitable for temperate growing conditions

Bisan begs for the planes drop their supplies in Northern Gaza where people starve in record numbers

—In 2008, the "watermelon wedge" is the 59th emoji approved by The Unicode Technical Committee, in between the peach and the question mark

A numbness settles over everyone I know

—A flag

A battle cry

never again – Linda M. Crate (she/her)

there is nowhere
safe to go,
and yet i still see people
talking about hamas and hostages;

as if this hasn't been happening
for decades—

beheaded babies,
children bombed and others
dying of starvation;

when is it enough?

i feel drained and exhausted,
and just when i think there's nothing
more terrible that israel can do
they somehow manage to trump my
worst expectations;

i cannot remain silent—

never again
is supposed to mean
never again for
anyone.

Twenty Years of Failures – **Clare Bayard** (she/he/they)

> *We will be greeted as liberators*
> —Dick Cheney, 2003

1.

Walking unblasted sidewalks in my intact shoes
in this land of dominators, I remember 2003.
That last March night was a six-month-long night
before the invasion of Baghdad. Some of us
stayed up all night for half a year, shaping
and training thousands of people into a body
that could shut down a city. Our wet cheeks raw
on the Financial District pavement.
The impossibility of that moment.

The days before the nineteenth of March,
the day after, the next twenty-one years.
What does it matter. How many times
did scraps of endless grief exit my body
in cubes of shower walls, echoes
of feral holler. Not many. I cage it.
Mostly we failed. Unmeasurably.

The anchor said: *Oh when you see the Shock and Awe you'll know it!*
The tickertape ran: *WE FED THEM HELL AND DEATH AT THE GATES*

2.

Thirty thousand people sheltering
in Al-Shifa Hospital when the soldiers entered.
The world is still allowing this. We grasp
for a firmament far above our fists.
Every day we choose primordial violence.
In this century of future mourning,
agape trampled like cornstalks
spit from the combine in a furious blaze,
I carry their names in my teeth.

3.

We say we are nervous and
love each other.
We call in the lions.
Dazed in billows
of blood. What
would you give to end
this disaster?

Accidental kin, I have come again
to ask anger, what do you love?
What is found where you begin?

In the Catacomb of Forgetting – Myfanwy Williams (she/her)
—Dedicated to the young Oud player of Rafah

So, in this catacomb of inevitable forgetting,
which cairn corridor remains fused with stone—
Solomon's memory palace, memoriam verborum
the ruins of Carthage, Alexandria burning blue
pity the soldier with our tax dollar trained
to the precipice of unhuman.

In the archive that bridges the dead and the living
a manifest of wedding ring, molars crowned with resin,
how the architecture of the skull betrays their son's grin
redolent against a portrait upon the Gazan shore.
Or the accoutrements of aging: shattered bifocals,
pacemaker pulsing upon a chamber collapsed.

Child, there is no safe place, and no one is coming
and today there is a good chance you will die,
as your mother and father and sister and brother
before you. So, listen from the reverberate caverns
that lie beneath the slaughterhouse rebranded
as holiday houses for the ignorant and glib.

Forgetting is cheap mercy and if you shall grow
to full height and adult longing, if you should wed,
curse the soldiers who gut memory for glory,
eschew the supple hands of salesmen selling
sandcastles from unmarked graves and listen
for the dexterous hands upon the fretless Oud.

Child crouching in the catacombs of forgetting,
know there is that which evades all verbiage,
that which the act of saying will bifurcate tongue.
Yet listen for those who tune memory into cadence
who from lamentation, from the dance of keening,
strum civilisation still.

not home – Salem Paige (they/them)

tired of
running and
running
just a breath and
stretch of cloth between

us did the air get colder,
then? you surely

never felt it, warm-
blooded and regular

how much gin
before the garden
dies? how many

breaths of this cold

air is there nowhere sacred—

rails of light on
the iron fence

geometric; square

the glow from
my indoors,
not your haven

A Stillborn Law – Savannah Jade (she/her)

still, still, still the room
where women come to plea,
testimony, testimony, testimony, testimony
the court-womb births two bleeds.

officials sacrifice a woman
in/an order to birth a new little woman
born naïve of her reversable skin
(child-mother; mother-child).

it's their Still Born Law:
rip child-mother inside out,
shove The Yellow Wallpaper down her throat like yolk.
"What came first? The chicken or the egg?"
lawyers give testaments about murder
and revelations about life. So many voices
drowning out the noise of the woman
that's choking.

she's choking.

still. they transmute her skin into a raincoat, a bulletproof vest,
a silk blanket, a wardrobe of sheathes protecting the baby in the
belly— this sword—piercing out of her into the Red Sea unwillingly
instead of rip-pl-ing in a manger across the ocean blue
into the hands of a Shepard who could grant more life
to a babe than she ever could.
but the White lightHouse won't baptize her with Choice
she must hiccup this red-plague law onto
            the next little woman
                    who slices through mother-child's own flesh
            turning her inside out again

before the court womb
when it's the next child-mother's turn
to ask for a surgeon's hanger
(still, still, still a sheathe).
And they'll watch mother's boat
wander with broken oars, in the dark,
row i n g   t o w a r d s   f r e e d o m
right off their shore, in plain view,
as it floods.

But no one will claim responsibility in this game of Clue.
(Mr. Red murdered Choice in the lighthouse using the Red Sea.)

Roe your boat
Wade goodbye
out of the womb, both to die
Readily, Red, red stream
life, for women, is but a dream.

A Slow Pour – **Erika Gill** (they/them)

A slow pour
a careful walk
wet leaf slip
machinery of a life

destructive deluge
shower of white phosphorus
dry dust rubble
machinery of genocide

awake in contrasts
anxiety behind a door
the door has been destroyed
and the hospitals
and the refugee camp

fences made poor neighbors
displaced, dying, dead.

dragging my cough in to wait
tables oblivious
that I could drop
sweet poison into open mouths
unfed

an engine of despair
devouring tracks laid
seventy five years deep

there is no bread
there is no bread

Recipe for Colonisation – **Zianna Ruiha** (she/they)

there's no need to preheat the oven
when instead
you could start by breaking down syllables
into hard ts & eliminate rhoticity
with your rs.
so we speak an english that is non-rhotic
& doesn't know the tongue of the land.

you then ban alcohol and infantilise in the northern territories,
with a heavy pen,
you vote no & celebrate january 26th,
you ignore voices and ignore data,
repeat that step on a quarterly basis.

you only listen to voices of a certain melanin tint,
you move & displace
beyond the spices on the rack,
then cut the umbilical cord that tethers,
Tangata whenua to Papatūānuku
this step engorges in march 1860
& will only continue to rise as you cook like your captain.

grow leaves from their dirt,
call it your cup of tea,
as you dice up the export market,
tax the food right out of the pantries
then pull the first loose thread of the finest fabrics
call your partition an act of kindness.
forget the asian blood spilt,
for her majesty's cup of tea,
it's part of the recipe
to bring out flavours of complicity.

then introduce foraging laws
for israelis to feast on greens,
as Palestinians starve in erasure
with a large fee for incarceration
you brand and sell the product of your colonisation
as a war,
& when there are whispers of
how could this be a war when only one has an army funded by the west?
just hush them with a spoonful of hummus.

now hurry,
at this simmering temperature you must fire explosive shells with
white phosphorous
every few days.
ban tik tok and public gatherings,
dilute the vote of the Kanak peoples,
send your military troops in.
these steps will halt resistance and prevent independence.

homes are destroyed,
indigenous land ownership is watered down,
past the moana.
language is attacked & revitalisation is criticised.
you drive them off till they're left to die
on no man's land.

commit a bison ecocide,
that nobody is prepared for.
do not respect the animal, only use the hide and tongue
as you mass-hunt
starve and drive off the indigenous peoples
off their land
it's now yours.

the umbilical cord that tethers
Tangata whenua to Papatūānuku
indigenous peoples to their land
in the most nurturing way
is repetitively
hacked &
butchered.

you now have colonisation
itemised on supermarket shelves,
on your dinner plate.
it will serve hundreds of millions
& don't worry about freezing it,
it never expires.

First published in Awa Wāhine Issue Ono

Cover Letter for a Dystopian Future – Arani Acharjee (she/her)

Dear humanity,
We are voracious troops of an unhinged species.
Our 24k gluttony-plated soul thrives on leftovers of brutality.
We burn cities and everything in between, the incense of charred
carcasses finds its way home or whatever is left of it.
Withering flowers under undead debris, their plea never reaches the
surface.
We set the stage with artillery smoke, and our footprints trail in
shades of scarlet—
call it a gesture of uprooted civility!

The young saplings who knew no sky, the raining shells have buried
them alive.
We wouldn't know if they slept through the lullaby.
Yet, we spit poison to earth's bosoms, for the seeds in winter, for the
birds on ground.

Oh humanity! what power do you hold in this playground of
malignancy?
we pierce, we gnaw, we savour, we devour!
but your finite eyes can't reach the mouth.
for you, there's always matcha in day, war at night.

Do you ever choke on a powerless sip?
When there's a mirror on your face, dead offspring at your feet?
Have you breathed air heavier than lead?
like a poet would say, "if there's hell in my world, all martyrs would've
survived…"

We, the predators of a dystopian world, have built our nest with
slaughtered skin and vines of gut.
We feed on your fear, we feed on your rage.
And the echoes of your weaponized paper—

save them for when your bubble becomes cage,
save them when your sky tumbles down.
Sincerely,
The breached souls of failed humanity

What justice do we seek as we continue to fail as humans?
How long does the genocide trail go as we outstretch the bloody claws
of history into a terrifying dystopia?

of olives and watermelon in October – Sebastian Ellios (he/him)

What do you know of bombs? This question—
        as much a throughline as a spectre. A most reliable
        haunting.

What do you know of bombs? It stands
        behind me while peering back from each face I encounter.
        I hear it in every "How are you?"
        What do you know of bombs?

And so I researched their physics—
        the implications of varying angles of entry
        on a blast radius and its crater.
I looked up their model numbers——GBU-31s and MK-82s,
        reminiscent of the appliance manuals
        stacked in my kitchen drawer.
I read of the inverse relationship between gravity acting upon them
        and the rise of Lockheed Martin stock
        on a ticker in Lower Manhattan.
I imagined the weight
        of rubble and the extraction
        of bodies, wondering
        how many might still
        be intact. How vivid red
        blood becomes against ashen skin.
        And I thought of children again and again.
        What do you know of bombs?

I know the sound of my best friend's laughter
        and that when she tries to stop it, she covers her mouth
        more with her wrist than her hand.
        I know the casualties climbed past 2,000
        on her birthday this year.

I know the honey brown of her eyes
        across so many tables we have shared
        and to leave out the smoked paprika when we cook.
        I know the casualties were approaching 3,000
        on her mother's birthday, just two days later.
I know the throw of her shoulders
        when we circle each other on a dance floor
        and how her curls bounce when we scream to "Mr.
        Brightside".
        I know the Canary Mission has kept a running prohle on her
        since she was 16, linking her advocacy
        to anti-Semitism and terrorism in an attempt
        to publicly decry her name;
        it is the first search result tied to her;
        it was last updated 4 days ago.
        What do you know of bombs?

I know my Laila.
        I know I am changed by her.
        And I know this world can never be short on beauty
        because she has existed within it.
        What do you know of bombs?

I know they are falling.
        On Gaza. God, I know they are falling.

Behind a refugee – O.P. Jha (he/him)

Watching the dusty creases
on the old bed-sheet,
finding no one for rejoicing a meal
at the dining-table
and blankness on the street,
a soldier whispered
some birds flown once
never returned again

with the fall of a house
an epoch ended
but the aggressors came
to crush seeds in the soil
and withered flowers on the land again.

The Horror in Their Eyes – **Dr. Adam Yaghi** (he/him)

"At least 283 corpses are found in a mass grave at Naser Hospital in Khan Yunis. The UN Human Rights Chief said, 'he is absolutely horrified.'"

Kay Burley: Who do you think those bodies are?
Fleur Hassan-Nahoum: Probably terrorists. . . .

Kay Burley: How do you think these people died?
Fleur Hassan-Nahoum: In gun battles with Israel.

Bulldozers are humming in the distance
inside Naser Hospital.

Imagine.

Imagine gasping for air
buried under mountains
of rubbish.

Imagine your chest
caving in
each time you exhaled.

Imagine clawing at debris,
to open a fissure
of hope
—to breathe.

Imagine the flicker in your eyes
darkening slowly,
slowly,
slowly,
—until no more.

The flow of time stops.

Only flashbacks.

Imagine.

Imagine watching soldiers
skin your child alive.

Imagine them
laughing
at her fish-like
twitching
and flapping
mutilated body.

Imagine them taking turns
raping a legs-amputated girl
in front of her father
before shooting both in the head.

She was 12.

"The experience was phenomenally exotic," they said to the camera.

Imagine the same soldiers
herding starved dogs
to feast on an old woman's body.

Imagine them fighting over her,
ripping her body apart from limb to limb.

Imagine the horror visible in their eyes—
they who have been turned into this monstrosity.

Imagine.

Imagine doctors,
hands tied behind their backs. . .

Imagine the hands.
Imagine . . .

*Kay Burley: "Why do you think some of the bodies were
found with ties around their hands?"*
*Fleur Hassan-Nahoum: "Well, because we probably
arrested the terrorists."*
Kay Burley: "And then killed them?"

Not Just a Brisket – Crystal Rivera (they/she)

          but a sorrow.
A lacquered-out tomorrow with fallen-outs.
I'm blocking out tomorrow for fallen-outs cause
there is a ceasefire that hasn't happened yet.
A ceasefire that *has* to happen, yet
I'm an anti-semitic jew for saying,
in kneeling-down position,
     not in my name.

Not just a brisket. A self-taught jew.
Puerto Rican-Russian jew.
A jew of color whose dishes have flavors of
sofrito y sazón so that
being Puerto Rican isn't a side-note
during our 8 days
       of Light.

But on this Hanukkah, what light do you speak of?
It is not just a brisket, but a sound.
   Listen.
     Younger me
wanted to make protest
the quietest way possible,
       like wood.
But not when you can hear the death of an olive tree,
as loudly as the genocide of its people.

And when blood family sits here and tells me
this is Jewish value, that *this*—murdering
entire family lines from their trees– isn't
making our ancestors weep

Oh honey,
   not in my fuckin' name.

Drop of tear in Ocean – Mahnoor Ali (she/her)

I got a fire igniting your kind inside my chest and within me

Can't tell how that fire is blazing my every single drop of flesh

Have your ever went through the flickering flames that casted long shadows?

Oh, neglected ones!

Only a mystic understands the blazing flames inside the spirit of mysticisim

My tongue is sealed with hundreds of locks

I got such furtive secret flare and gleaming flames that they can consume both of the worlds

Have you ever burned like fire?

Did it cool down? Turn into white and blue flames?

Let tears keep flowing from my eyes, let them never stop

Let my heart bleed until failure—what is its use if it's does not contain humanity?

Why would I keep my head (on my shoulders) from now on?

What I drink is a blood of liver,

What I eat is trouble and sorrow,

Since you have set me ablaze from inside and outside;

The burden of grief I carry cannot be endured by destiny itself...

None like me has seen in this valley of suffering

If all trees turn into pens and all oceans become ink,

They'd cry n wail for the bloodshed to end and beg God to give freedom to the wounded bird

Oh Abraj!

There's no remedy for this sorrow until my death

No surprise if my tears add up to become ocean and seas

The grief still won't be enough...

The Delusion of Humanity – Julissa Beltran (she/her)

The smoke of your blown out candle
has fabricated wishes.
The way the white lace travels
through the wind is our dying hope.

Fingers trace our tombstones and
claw them open in an innocent daydream.
Sobs continue to drown in themselves.
The tank crushing my chest.
Winning.
The world letting it win.

The smoke wields a world where ashened flesh and
hollow cheeks are what the youth play with.
A place where limbs never fail to be replaced.
The loss of an organ never without stock yet
there is a blockade to what pumps humanity.

In the noises that escape your lips, we miss if
there is a bud between your words.
Searching,
the rotting plaster of those dolls
look more like you
than what they were made of.

**Insufficient Words for Gravity (The Occupation of Bombs) –
Meredith MacLeod Davidson** (she/they)

Bombs are falling—no—
       they are thrown: formed by hands
       cupped into the shape of destruction
       and heated in the kiln of cruelty

Bombs are dropping—no—
       they've been launched: prepared by a colonizing body
       like a rocket, an entire platform built for this galvanizing
       a hundred camera lenses all to witness the missile fragment a
       shared sky

Bombs have been given
       as with blankets, or malware—a trojan horse
       striking violence on a people

Bombs have been manufactured,
       are being manufactured for the roil of profit
       destruction of homes: a shrapnel scrapping souls
       language stolen, leeched with
       the land, with the lives

The language of gravity becomes injury when stolen in service of war. But in the same way that a people still exist despite their attempted erasure, ideas retain merit despite the exploitation of their naming, no matter the oppressor's imposition, the language of liberation cannot diminish.

Bombs are falling—no—Bombs are dropping—no—
Bombs are given with closed hands
Bombs are manufactured without consent
Bombs cannot drop, dropping is for tears and rain.
Bombs cannot fall, falling is for empires.

Bravery in Silence – Zehnab Hayat (she/her)

Bravery, that's the only word that comes to mind,
To stand against evil in a world that would rather be blind.
We, the people commend you, strong and profound,
Showing us that humanity in even the darkest of room can be found.

In your actions, hope is found, a
beacon so bright,
A guidance of resilience, a star
in the night.
In silent protest, you raised
your sign,
A gesture simple, yet
heartbreakingly divine.

No words were spoken, yet a message so clear,
More impactful than the speeches that captivated the mere,
A criminal's rhetoric, hollow and cold,
Dwarfed by your bravery, an action so bold.

Silence roared loud than deceitful claims,
Exposing the truth, extinguishing a never-ending flame.
With an unwavering heart, you held your ground,
And in that moment, a true hero was found.

Thank you for giving us hope,
I nearly let go,
But now,
I'll hold on,
A little tighter.

it doesn't – Linda M. Crate (she/her)

even as a kid
i found the
"chosen ones"
narrative really weird,

because weren't we
all chosen to live here
on earth for whatever reason?

but i see now it was just the justification
to do cruel, unspeakable things to people

whose land they wanted to colonize;

how many children have to die
before someone says: ENOUGH with
their full and entire chest?

i'm horrified just hearing the information,
cannot imagine how people in this situation
even hang on with any threads of hope;

but they are strong and they are beautiful—

& i hope that soon there will be a
ceasefire,
because how hard-hearted do you have
to be to watch children, mothers, and fathers
die without having a shred of empathy
or compassion?

how does a nation defend itself by bombing
churches, hospitals, and universities?

it doesn't.

All That We Carry – **Myfanwy Williams** (she/her)
—From Gadigal (Sydney) to Gaza

I)   THE WEIGHT

Listen, the bones that remain heave
with the weight of Their Chosen-ness,
and even our pale retinas descend
in gravitational witness.

Watch, a sack slung on his shoulder,
the teen returning god his smiles
his brother's body balancing
in pieces along his spine.

The bag is not heavy, he claims.
Why should it be heavy?
He was my little brother.
And I loved him.

II)   HOW WE CARRY

This life is one of always carrying,
rucksack pressing into scapula,
nerves pinched and discs slipped.

Or vertebrate upon vertebrate,
balancing woven baskets
on our crowns, sturdy.

And the trick is one of distribution,
to assist in long haul carriage,
so, the weight bearer can continue.

The survivors carry remnants
of their dead in garbage bags,
striving for unleavened ground.

Perhaps this is plastic's sole virtue:
to preserve the blood that holds us,
when the ground capsizes.

My Sister – Ramona McCloskey (she/her)

My mother's womb never gave me a sister
Yet I do have one — she lives in faraway land
We have never met, nor do we know
Each other's name or deepest fears

We do not understand each other's tongue
Yet I can hear her words clearly
And the small fragrant leaves of zaatar
Understand her when she whispers

We do not look the same
Her silky hair is tucked under a cover
But if the wind tried to blow her veil away
I'd hold onto it for as long as she needs

My sister lives in the land of oranges
And olive trees that overlook the sea
But her sons do not sleep at night
Like mine do, safe in warm beds

Her husband does not come home
After a hard day's work, like mine does
Her husband lies under the rubble
Of what was once her family home

My sister, my sons too live in an occupied land
Only I was blessed to be able to fight
For their freedom with my pen and my voice
Not forced to do it with my flesh and my bones

My sister, I will repeat your words until my throat goes dry
Even to those who listen to no one but themselves
Until your sons are able to hear the birds
And pick the oranges and olives that grow free
For my sister's name is not a noun
My sister's name is a verb

Intramural – **Ashley Fish-Robertson** (she/her)

To sit behind the pane is nice,

but to feel the sun on your face

is to prove infinity in even

the smallest of moments

and in the naivest of

creatures

memorial to a village – Derek R. Smith (he/him)
—a braided poem after "Your Village" by Elana Bell
and "We Deserve a Better Death" by Mosab Abu Toha

In a village there are people
          those who hope

In a village there are bodies
          those who were

There are broken walls
     and broken dreams
          and broken memories
in a village

There are broken wristwatches
     scattered glass face cracked apart like
          slices of melon enjoyed here last summer
in this very village
when it was a living place-
a place for life
a butterfly doesn't know this place is done
     and flutters by without passing judgment

Kittens rest here post-violence, those who did nothing but be born
     here in this village
          later they pay for some other cat's aggressions

In a village there are flipping faded photographs
     these shells of a well-rounded life
          these rounds of shells that fell life
            these discards

Because they aren't your photographs, not your wristwatch,
                    because your dream isn't done
                              and your nephew is still very much alive

You watch some b-roll on tv
your loungechair is too lumpy, your neighbor's dog is still barking.
                    your mind almost wonders who lived here
                              in this televised village wasteland,
                                        you pause before considering
                                        your village could be next
yet it won't be
'cause people know how to pronounce your village
and if you disappeared,
someone would organize a search party

                    and in the case of the worst
                    your gravestone would be error-free
                    established in a classic, weighty slatey fonted
marble
                    with someone who remembers flowers
                    or someone who had paid for them to be placed

there's a quote loosely about a thousand deaths a statistical
phenomenon
                    and your one life lost a tragedy;

                              your village is too small.
                                        it always was.

Audience – Devon Webb (she/her)

We, unwitting audience of genocide
immobile
in our glass houses
where all the stones bounce back
& clatter to our streets
where the only pockmarks
are the potholes
we blame our pussy
government for

Meanwhile
an incomprehensible amount
of miles away
innocents are bombed every minute
why are we not
waging war against this holocaust
is it because they are not white
I do not understand such
selective politics
I do not understand such
lack of humanity

What a privilege to continue
how ironic it feels that
here, nothing changes
war crimes before our eyes but
our eyes are screens & we have
wifi & electricity
but put our phones away for
mental health reasons
when we see hospitals collapsing

as if we'd rather be blind than
see ourselves do nothing.

Ghosts – Leo Rose Rodriguez (they/them)

What is the death knell of a city? When its houses are gone, when its name is changed,
when the map is whitewashed over? Does a nation die when policy declares it never-born?
When a flag   is banned at barrel-point,   then its colors, can you stop us
from seeing it in   red petals   and green stems?   If   we cannot say
                    a name,   can we be stopped   from   hearing   it   in
the wind?   And will the chanters
            be silent,   with no name   to invoke?   How
a thing lives   on in   the space   it   leaves.

Times – Terri McCord (she/her)

Out of order x ten
        the bathrooms, the talkers,
the numbers, the soda machines,
the wireless internet   the restaurants
during COVID, the immune systems x
millions, the businesses x thousands   gone under
        the mouths that mouth, they do
do they, if only you, or I, could
hear them   order   out of
take an order   write it down
finger it   push the buttons   deliver
the order   order
the gavel, the strike, judgement x five men
out of order   the bears in the
parking lots, the rockets in the
neighborhoods, the fence lines that border
no border, no order   the playground slides
that go nowhere
the temperatures
that bounce, the lit fuses that fly back
back into the houses

Born to Atone – Genevieve Chornenki (she/her)
         —Al-Shifa Hospital, 2023

My God, she is forsaken.
None intercedes on her behalf.
The Pontius Pilates wash their hands
and do not even ask, what evil has she done?
See ye to it is their silent chant.

Fresh from the womb scarce taken,
transparent manger for a bed,
her term abrupt. So small
and yet no comfort on her mother's shrivelled breast;
an early taste of vinegar with gall.

Her people cower, shaken,
poured like water though none be,
nor food nor light nor heat.
Her brother whimpers, will my toys still be alive?[2]
Her cross of girders, smoke and dust, concrete.

The Pontius Pilates wring their hands,
and do not dare to ask, what evil has she done?
See ye to it still their wordless chant.

And what of he, the Liege Lord of creation
who thrusts the cup into wee fists
unable to say no?
May generations hold him to account on her behalf,
reproach the unearned suffering he imposed.

---

[2] See "Younger Than War" by Mosab Abu Toha, *The Atlantic*, November 9, 2023.

NICU – Leo Rose Rodriguez (they/them)

Just another day, *habibti*.
I know it's cold.
I know mama is gone,
and to pull air into tadpole lungs
      is trying to chain the sun
      with fishing nets of baby-thin hair.

You will know the sky
as a blaze, the ground
as a fine dust of cement and bone,
faces only as bloody
and pickled with exhaustion
if you grow up—
which you must.

I whisper a lullaby
over the explosion.
Just another day, *habibti*.

Will the World Do Nothing? – Prudence Brooks (she/her)
   —a quote from Bisan Owda

the rain makes a pattering sound on the pavement
like a carefree child skipping home from school,
but the children do not go to school anymore.

a bloodied Palestinian boy
carries the limp body of a friend,
drenched in white phosphorus,
through the flooded streets of Gaza,
searching for a place to bury him.

Israel uses chemicals of war like they are baking ingredients,
as if they were dipping kids in powdered sugar,
preparing to put them on a platter for everyone to feast.

like anything about this could be sweet.

they said *move south; you will be safe there.*
but there is no safe place in a genocide.

they say the tigers come at night,
but the tanks come on the holidays.
not in the stealth of the quiet,
but under the cover of the noise.

you cannot hear a mother's mournful howl
over the sound of a roaring stadium.
the world goes wild for a touchdown
and somewhere in Rafah,
another mosque falls.

Birthing Generations – Savannah Jade (she/her)

Young   salmon   swimming   upstream
                                          Booming
                        hummingbirds
            flying
backwards

humans sharing
beds   before
    hearts

isn't nature so wonderfully cruel
to turn dysfunction into survival?

not in my name – **Lyss Stainer** (they/them)

because my body remembers you,
beneath the warsaw smog.
not running away but running towards
a future where persecution wasn't your only lover,

the dizzying melody of circular histories—
wound still fresh, fear not as warning
but instead as loaded weapon.
i have become the armed accomplice to your greatest nightmares

for a city burns, and my ancestors flesh
has been loaded as the ammunition.
somewhere in this burning night
my pain is fuel to keep the fire ablaze.

how much damage is enough damage to quench
power hungry oil barons?
how much damage is enough damage
to rebuild concentration camps and call them safety?
it's predictable, the rationalization of evil, the knife through a cheek
this makes destruction seem more like tradition.

i'm told what seems like genocide is often genocide,
that the weapons funded from my tax dollars
are engraved with my initials.
in my dreams of palestine,
it is early morning
the sun blazing over the regrowth of olive trees
the clear sky embracing a people back to their homeland.

We are all interwoven. Standing in solidarity with the ancient stones I weave LOVE FOR ALL. I weave to remember the oneness of us all. I weave to call an end to the killing, to the harm being done to the people of Palestine, to the land and beings, and so to us all. I weave for FREEDOM FOR US ALL.

—Tor Purrett (she/her)

Obligation – Clare Bayard (she/he/they)

> *— nods to my chosen family of conscientious objectors, from Israel to the U.S. and beyond, who choose prison and other deprivations over military conscription and participation in occupations and invasions.*

The colors of the soldiers' eyes are not different. They too eat apricots in stone fruit season. They say they are just following orders. Some enlist every muscle, every sweeping sheet of fascia to forge their body's collection of angles and possible directions into a molded self which may apply its energies towards a particular transformation.

What enrolls a body in the coming-of-age story that extracts concrete-flecked red underwear from rubble to mount as trophy on your tank? What causes a twenty-year-old boy to climb into the crib of a child displaced to the "safe area" his unit will bomb tomorrow? What must you forget to photograph yourself cuddling their stuffed animals, limbs intact?

Some of them embrace the gun like they were taught, but a few of them refuse, just like here. I remember teenagers on the bus in Tel Aviv knocking me aside, M-16s slung along their hips over their drop-waisted uniforms, insouciant like any teenager, child soldiers trained like any child soldier.

Hey Pal: – Zeid (he/they)

Last year I lost my jedo – to many: a pal
This year I lose cousins and cousins of a pal

Here in the United States, there's the half-joke
"Fireworks or gunshots?" I'd smirk towards a pal

Teta – jedo's – recites Your climb to God's Mountain
Raised from the rocks is a statue of You, old pal

Here the shops sell large fruits shrunk to 'personal size' yet
Watermelon is best enjoyed shared with a pal

Child baba used to avoid the Jordan River
Half-jokes don't resurrect the dead ears of a pal

Here my coworker suffered from some falsities
Telling lies aimed to bring her against You, my pal

Adult baba attended my cousin's baptism
Dipped in waters that submerged the Nazareth pal

Here a boss excused racism for her career
Half-joke politicians desecrate our dear pal

Teta, for breakfasts, pled love to her grandchildren
Plates upon plates upon plates upon plates from pal

Here I once brought watermelon to a function
The red lid squashed all to a mush; I'm sorry, pal

Jedo lives in cited accounts of Your history
Yet lived a pilgrimage away from our old pal

There You will find the gift of a magic carpet
Bombing sealing ceiling-shaped corks above Your pal

Me: I would never know You outside of accounts
Written in the crosswinds by truant pal and pal

You: Dammi min-ak bas ma ba'a raf-ak, Rashid
Shoo a'am-el ghir ma ahki el half-jokes, hobi

You: دمي منك بس ما بعرفك , Rashid
شو أعمل غر ما أحكي الhalf-jokes، حبي

يوو: دمي منك بس ما بعرفك، راشد
شو أعمل غر ما أحكي الهالف جوكس، حبي

*First published in Rising Phoenix Review

for blooming – O.P. Jha (he/him)

the moon, above the thick bedspread
of hypocrite clouds that pretend to be
the mothers of showers but floating furiously
with the soul of smoke and the body of havoc,
looks like an expression suffocating in the corridors
of spoilt and rotten similes and metaphors,
watches the Earth as a grandma, in a deserted home
near the Dnipro, looks silent as a defunct tank
bruised by Russian missiles, where the Dnipro is willing
to talk to sunflowers but seems reluctant to lick
the smoke marks and wounds on split glasses
ready to slip from the panes of half burnt houses

the moon is searching a crack in the clouds
for talking the orphan date-trees in Gaza strip
it's willing to see its reflections on the chest
of the Mediterranean
and refractions on the palms of children getting ready
to be refugees soon
but there's no orifice in the realm of smokes

between the trees and the sea, there're sand-dunes
that have stopped whispering on the back of wind

till the setting of the Venus, the morning star
the moon is ready to wait
for the rising of lost souls

as the captain of patience much above
the web of chaos, the moon understands
fake clouds will never rain
one day, they'll disintegrate,
some seeds will germinate, grow, rise, prosper
and bloom as flowers on the soil.

Birthright – **Anna Zilbermints** (she/her)

At eighteen years old,
I couldn't bring myself to swallow
the Advil, even the glass of water
next to it made my stomach roll over
in (what honestly felt like) its grave.

The air mattress that tried rejecting me
all night
suddenly wouldn't let me go. I tried
telling it the spins
were over, but it knew
better, and I was comforted by
its lack of judgement I knew I would get

when my family returned
and found me in the same position
I was in when they left
a few hours ago.

Of course, for years after, they wouldn't let me forget
        That Time I Skipped the Bahá'í Gardens™
but what was an eighteen-year-old to do
in Israel for the first time
at her cousin's open bar wedding?

        Yes, this was the hangover from hell in the holy land.

A definition of birthright is
any right or privilege to which a
person is entitled by birth
pretty straightforward so I
wasn't too worried. I still had
years to cash in on the free trip
I was promised in exchange for
memorizing a Torah portion
when I was twelve that I'd
forget by the time I was
thirteen.

A definition of entitlement is
belief that one is deserving of or
entitled to certain privileges
we're all familiar but
we're talking about a land
whose language I never learned
soil I'd never stepped on air I'd
never breathed until I was in a
fetal position
debating whether the headache
or nausea would kill me first:

These definitions were starting to feel oddly
interchangeable.

I have danced too many times on soil taken
by force, and I wonder how many
native graves I've disrespected
in drunk revelry without even realizing.

How long can I really live
trying to pry away
the blood-crusted hands clasped over my ears
to the sounds of screams
begging to just be heard?   I want to hear them.

Ignorance may be bliss,
but it's not protection

and I can't begin to explain how
I don't want to swallow the
shame I rightfully feel when
stomping along the stolen ground
anymore.

It hits too close to home.

I still haven't been back to Israel.

can you? – Linda M. Crate (she/her)

decades of brutality,
countless lives
stolen;

each person was someone's
world—

each person was a
universe full of hopes,
aspirations, dreams,
laughter, joy, sorrow,
anger, pain, and humanity;

now reduced to dust—

how can anyone
justify something so brutal
and so cruel?

i don't want my tax dollars
going toward hurting someone else,
of robbing parents of their children or
children of their parents or siblings;

why can't my tax dollars feed
the starving people in my own country?
or house the homeless? or give teachers
fair pay?

why does my country fund israel?

i cannot turn away from the
outrage or the pain of palestine,
can you?

Steps of Hope – **Eman Alhaj Ali** (she/her)

Two steps: one, two,
Swing wide the door,
A new dawn's order, a new world to explore!
Fleeing fast, through fog and fear,
From bustling blocks to barren spheres,
Tent to tent, in twilight's dread,
Haunted by shadows, lost hopes thread.
Pale faces in the plumes of dust,
Sorrowful screams, in silence, we trust.

Crowded corners, chaos reigns,
Pregnant pauses, they bear the pains.
Beneath the blazing, burning sun,
Shaking, shuddering, the race is run.
To stay or fly, the night brings fright,
Missiles wail a woeful plight.

Water whispers a distant dream,
While food fades, a fragile theme.
From north to south, the struggle flows,
With costly tools that nobody knows.
From harsh winter to autumn's chill,
This is the life of Gazans, still.
Twelve months, in the grip of strife,
Two steps: one for the future,
Two for the shadows of a shattered life.

Eager eyes edged with echoing dread,
Each child's cry carving hope into the bed.
Evacuation orders dance like phantoms,
Evoking fears that feel like a tantrum.
Families fractured, forever unfurled,
In this fraught, fragmented world.
Displacement drags its heavy hand,
As dreams dissolve like grains of sand.

Amidst the horrors that loom and leer,
The ghostly grip of relentless fear.
Time ticks treacherous; the clock creeps slow,
Each second a reminder of what we forgo.
Hearts hammer hard in the hushed cacophony,
Lost in the labyrinth, aching to be free.

Rubble reigns where once there was life,
Memories mingle with the echoes of strife.
Crimson stains the ground, stories untold,
Embers of yesterday's warmth turn cold.
In a world where warmth seems to elude,
Walls weep, remembering laughter imbued.

Yet from the ashes arise voices bright,
Calling for courage to ignite the night.

"We are not conquered, nor will we bow,
We'll forge a path; we will rise somehow."
So we take these steps, burdened yet bold,
In the grip of despair, we'll refuse to fold.

Two steps: one, two,
With whispering winds, let resilience renew.
Though shadows stretch and hardships loom,
Hope flickers softly amidst the gloom.
Together we'll navigate through sorrow and strife,
Holding on tightly to the threads of life.
For every step on this fragile street,
Brings us closer to healing, one heart, one beat.

At Dawn, the Flour Massacre – Clare Bayard (she/he/they)

Flour is grain ground to transport the sun
from the stalk that collected sun, makes body from
light. Sun stretches the round-bellied
wheat berry milled into powder to fill stomachs,
fuel the mitochondrial engines of the cells
that move our limbs, bellow our lungs,
commute our blood through our bodies
doing its work of renewing life

Tanks opened fire
on hundreds of shirts
on starving people
rushing to the first
food truck entering
the north of Gaza
in weeks. People
have been eating
sand, sleeping in the streets
awaiting these trucks.
Forced starvation
screws on silencers.

*"Their blood was mixed with the flour. The mothers and sisters, the
families, will never bake that flour. Will never bake that bread. They
will never get back their homes. They said goodbye to their families
to get that food and they will never eat that food."*

— reportage from Gaza by Palestinian journalist
Bisan Owda on February 29 2024.

What Gaza Taught Me – Corey Stano (they/them)

In the revolution you must cry
every sorrow should rain from your eyes
to feed your righteous spirit

In the revolution you must laugh
raise your fractured voice in joy
to dishearten the tormentors you face

In the revolution you must
dance and sing
love and scream
paint and write
hunger and dream

In the revolution you must remember:
your humanity is a weapon
your oppressor cannot possess

A Lemon Tree, 5 Chickens, and a Rooster – Dr. Adam Yaghi
(he/him)

Place: Haifa

"Quiet! We're shooting,"
an MP orders a small crowd
gathered hastily.

"STOP the holocaust in Gaza."
"STOP the genocide."
"Stop killing children" and "life for Gaza" screams a mother.
"Bring back our soldiers," yells another.

"Disperse or else!"

An old couple, passing by, wonders, "what the heck!"
"Arabs or Jews?" The woman asks. "Because I don't speak to dirty
Arabs. And if Jews, then 'shut up you morons! We're shooting!"
--The man? Well, he egged them. Just like that.
Precisely 5 eggs because he thought 7 should be enough to make
her
favorite rum cake.

Place: Tel Al Rabie

Thousands dance and sing.
"Gaza is a graveyard," they cheer, and "there will be no school
tomorrow in Gaza. . .
. . . no school ever,
. . . no children are left in Gaza."

They cheer for a soldier,
a sniper,
a pilot of a jetfighter.

The kill: babies,
children,
pregnant women,
mothers,
grandmothers,
grandfathers,
sisters,
brothers,
nieces,
nephews,
great nieces,
great nephews,
38 families, 5 generations,
and thousands more.
All gone....

They cheer!
They still cheer!

They cheer for a new Hiroshima,
. . . a Nagasaki,
. . . for genocide Joe,
. . . for the U.S.A.
They cheer for more blood, more stolen land, more resources. . . .
They cheer for racial purity.
They cheer for apartheid superiority.
They cheer for genocide and ethnic cleansing of all of Palestine.

Place: Diaspora

I am the Indian of Palestine.
Should I be angry?

In Gaza, I have a house,
a family,
friends,
memories,
a lemon tree,
5 chickens and a rooster,
white pigeons,
a gray cat,
shattered hopes,
and growing despair.

Like many of my kind,
I wait
at the Western gate
of hell
for the gatekeepers
to usher me in.

In America, I have always been the Other
—the Biblical Goliath.
In Canada, I am the irrational, untamed barbarian from the East
—the obstacle delaying the Second Coming.
In Europe, I am a collateral damage,
or at best a humanitarian crisis
dying a slow, but painful, death.

Place: Gaza

I am the besieged.
I am the bereaved.
I am the displaced.
I am the maimed.
I am the starved.

I am the demonized.
I am the oppressed,
I am the dehumanized.
I am the colonized repelling against your supremacist genocidal
hate.
I am the victim of your original colonial sin.

I am witness to your crimes.
I am a freedom fighter.
I am a rebel.
I am the Indian of Palestine.

Shall I be angry?
It is natural to resist.

Bloom Where You're Planted – Elizabeth Day (she/her)

I get told this a lot
Because people only see me crying
Tears of grief over somewhere I'm not

But I've gone where the wind takes me
Ever since it blew me away
In a nourishing and strengthening storm
And told me to stop
In a seemingly barren patch of dirt
"Stop" the voice was firm
So I planted

And only good things have happened
To me ever since

All I do is bloom
So if you see me crying
Don't worry
It's part of the process
I bloom where I'm planted
But I have to water my seeds

Letters to Mahmoud – Myfanwy Williams (she/her)
—For Mahmoud Darwish, Palestinian poet and activist

I)   Brother, you were not the last of the resistance poets.
Even now you are meeting the freshly martyred bards
seated beneath an olive grove ensconced in the firmament,
debating verse and metre and form.

Let me tell if you of this 'here' place. Too many
images like shrapnel in the retinas, so you may
have missed the world awash with Keffiyeh
and watermelon. Now, even the Christians march
on a Sunday, and the Jewish youth have sewn
watermelons on their yamakas.

Brother, you were not the last of the resistance poets,
and even now we whisper *intifada*.
Our protest is now poetry:
our poetry now prayer.

II)   Brother, let me speak to you of a bird
you may not yet know. In my country
they are the size of a crow, with pink, grey
and white plumage, and crests on their heads -
eccentric kings stretching their natural reign.
I once saw such a bird, seated on a perch,
inside a long narrow cage. When first
caught, it had wounded its captors. and they
with the power of wording the world
labelled it Terror, labelled it Hateful,
charged it with wanting to destroy its captors
when simply it sought return to its
semi-arid land. Now it plucks its breast
and pink feathers fall to the prison

floor, skin raw and bloody, and sometimes
it sings and sometimes it dances when a child
brings her phone music to the cage doors,
and sometimes it dances to her Tik Tok tunes
because song is hard to pluck and song
does not know borders.

For Halima – Genevieve Chornenki (she/her)

I ask you friends, please don't avert your eyes.
Heed what ancient olive trees feel and see,
and pray for the means to salve the wounds, the cries.

No chance to bid her flocks, her fields goodbye,
so up above the table hangs a key.
I ask you friends, please don't avert your eyes.

Her plate of beans was laid out when the skies
exploded concrete, metal, dust, debris.
Oh, for the means to salve the wounds, the cries!

Sons, fathers, husbands squat with burning thighs.
No Shem, Japheth to veil their nudity.
I ask you friends, please don't avert your eyes.

White winding sheets, black lettering, string ties.
Four generations lost for all eternity.
Oh, for the means to salve the wounds, the cries.

The one who hears world sighs, does she take sides?
Or does the one who bids, come follow me?
I ask you, friend, please don't avert your eyes.
Had I the means, I'd soothe all wounds, all cries.

– Siege –
Daniel Schulz (he/him)

MEDICAL	–BOMB–	SUPPLIES
FOOD	–BOMB–	RATIONS
REFUGEE	–BOMB–	CAMPS
HOSPITAL	–BOMB–	FACILITIES
PARENTS	–BOMB–	CHILDREN
SAFETY	–BOMB–	ZONES
NEWS	–BOMB–	REPORTS

She is digging herself out – Meredith MacLeod Davidson
(she/they)

She is digging herself out
of the ground. And the slaughter
cleans, tours blood between limbs
split for one more knife trick.
The naked concrete bears another
miscarriage: a girl with stone upturned.

She is digging herself out of the ground.
And every empty soul birthed of the west
is questioned. At the gate explosives are placed
by hand with nothing left to lose—
lies streak naked, raw footage
and reason denied entry.

A flame licks from the conscience
of the complicit, the calls for life censured
through the walls of the house. America is a racist
nation—a hellfire missile spreading its blades to shred
shelters, to whittle a homeland to dust
a legacy with the consequence of terror.

The so-called subhuman rises from the press
of oblivion – the peoples' water is as good as tears.
Salt, sea, and the body particulate, you are suffocating
remembrance, the repressed and oppressed resident,
waters crash and recede; children go by something new
when no one in their family survives to tell them their names.

Gaza; buried under the rubble,
a Palestinian girl helps her rescuers.
She is digging herself out of the fucking ground.

Where Olives No Longer Grow – Grace R. Reynolds (she/her)

I drove home in the rain
watched leaves scatter on asphalt like
tiny birds fluttering in the wind. I wondered
      are there any leaves, trees, left in Gaza
      for someone to watch the breeze carry away?

The crunch of stems in hands, hands that cradle
dead babies. Mothers, fathers, they smell their children's burned
hair
one last time
      before placing their broken limbs in a white bag,
      zippers shielding eyes forever shut from skies dropping
hellfire and ash.

When I smell my baby's hair, kiss their face,
whirl them around in the sunshine, my heart cries
for all the parents who can no longer do that,
      no matter how old or young.
      A life is a life is a life.

What memories can be made when there are no trees
to block the sunshine on a hot summer's day?
Where olives no longer grow,
      no oil to set at a table no longer there,
for a family no longer there?

Letters – **Terri McCord** (she/her)
— Palestinian aid worker describes 'really dire' conditions
for those who have stayed in northern Gaza, CNN, 10-23-2023

The body   becoming
epistolary
thick, black ink written with care

and, perhaps, prescience,
the beginning of another kind
of love letter
in the face   of the not known,
the practice of writing out
a child's name
on the legs and abdomen
for identification
after airstrikes or being
lost and made unrecognizable

Here, a small sweater
label bears a first name
in block letters,
and the child has
forgotten the early morning coldness
is busy somewhere else.

After the Thunder Spoke – Yuna Kang (she/they/any)

i.

Is this how the summer rain of Starnbergersee feels? We

have run out of fisher kings and gods to steal—
and instead we hurtle,
newly-born,
towards the end of beginnings. The

night air is newly cluttered with droplets of weak fog—
but it is a warm July night. Things
lose their pattern, the shape and tethers of reality
are systematically weakening. We are living in an
end.

ii.

I browse the sunset orgies of East Bay desperation—
the clouds of autumn spooling out of cups like
women trying to find a place to go after
late-night flings with ill-intentioned lovers,
there is the diner boarded up and the tiles
sit over slumbering graves. I meet people
who leave, and then I leave, and I sit on
old benches at Ohlone park,
counting cigarette butts, wondering where the night goes.

iii.

When it's quiet, when it's dark, I strain to hear
the siren whispers of ancestors dead and alive, and
I don't know what to do. Or where to go.
Police cars scream by me like the wailing end—
And we are dying and dead and our world is yearning
to meet the never-ending sea.

v.

I lay in the foggy beds of half-strangers
in pinkish retreats, where the sun rises over
tulle canopies, and it is almost morning.
The moment of suspension and laughter and bruising and bone is
gone—
and I live for these after-moments, devoid of
delicious awkwardness and cunning.
The world enters the spaces where people now refuse to occupy.
(i can see their shadows still, imprintations
of dusky auras seeping into the atomic
structures of the furniture)
and I am quiet.

0.

We are all going to die—
and I wonder if this is what Heaven is like:
knowing, and loving, and hating, and laughing:
and living to be still.

remedy – Rowan Tate (she/her)

i improvise a body,
sewing together the dark fish
who ate the night out of the blood
of the women before me.
their lungs and stomachs,
which i've inherited,
i knead and mold
into fingers, the flat of a palm,
tendons, the delicate
wiring of worlds. skin grows back
so many histories later
in the shade of the people
we loved. in the grooves
of mortality, nouns
multiply and divide, bear
children who wear
your april yellow eyes.
whoever gave me my
breast and my belly
had her own bad dreams
but they are better now.
yam makes the liver less skittish.
i dry dandelion root and
nettles for tea to remember
the shape my grandmother took.
when you hold my hand,
you hold so many others.

AFTERWORD

Poetry soars above silence, poetry shatters ignorance, poetry flies into the space that is hope and light.

The poems in this anthology are a testament to the worst of times, to a genocide carried out in our own time. The voices raised to raise funds for Gaza are voices that will never be silenced.

These voices have been raised in the name of every poet that a tyrant army sought to crush. These poems keep words alive. They speak to the wrong of invasion, these words are the sword that crushes violence.

Poetry exists beyond walls. Poetry condemns megalomaniacs, it strikes against expansionism and extermination. This collection of poetry condemns the crime that is colonisation.

Poetry is the first word spun by a child and the last word gasped by a prophet of peace.

I commend this anthology to you, to be read, re-read, treasured and shared. This anthology is a store-house of wisdom and it is the strength of the spirit that rises in the harshest of times.

—Saige England
November 2024

ABOUT THE CONTRIBUTORS

- **Dr. Adam Yaghi**, a clinical associate professor at New York University in Shanghai, specializes in diasporic Arab(ic) and American literatures. He primarily investigates the intersections of religion, identity, and power. He has published on Muslim literature in North America, popular testimonial literature by Americans of Arab/Muslim descent, and Palestinian literature of resistance. He is a published Palestinian Canadian poet from the Gaza Strip, Palestine.

- **Alexandria Piette** (she/her/they/them), originally from Grand Rapids, is a resident of the Sunrise Side—or Oscoda, Michigan. They are the indie author of The Blazing Heart of a Moonlight Arsonist.

- **Anna Zilbermints**, (she/her) a daughter of Jewish immigrants, is a graduate of the University of Iowa in English and psychology. She is a poet of both the written and spoken word varieties.

- **Arani Acharjee** is an emerging writer from Kolkata, India. She is a Zoology graduate and wildlife lover. She has been passionate about writing since her pre-teen days. She has co-authored ten anthologies till date and published her solo book in 2021.

- **Ashley Fish-Robertson** (She/Her) is a journalist and poet based in Montreal. Her work has appeared in ROOM, Funicular, Soliloquies Anthology, The Encore Poetry Project Anthology, This Magazine and more.

- **Benjamin Eric** (he/him) is a Washington, DC based writer and Querencia author. He is a member of Democratic Socialists of America and Jewish Voice for Peace. An antiwar advocate, he writes about Palestine and has volunteered for advocacy organizations.

- **Carla Schick** is a queer educator, writer & activist for transformative justice, including decades of solidarity work for a free Palestine. Their writings can be found in Fourteen Hills, Colossus: Body and many other journals. They received a 2023 Poetry Award from Sf Foundation/ Nomadic Press.

- **Charlie Jasper** (they/he/she) is a TRANSdisciplinary artist, poet, and producer. They host a monthly poetry workshop & open mic, PARFAIT POETRY NIGHT as her drag alter ego Peach Bellini.

- **Chelsea Palermo** is a poet, intuitive & alchemist. She holds an MFA in Poetry from Drew University & was nominated Poet Laureate of Asbury Park, NJ. Her poems can be found in This Broken Shore, Ghost City Review, Soup Can, The Monmouth Review & more.

- **Clare Bayard** (she/he/they) is a writer, parent, and organizer who has been working for decades to end US empire, midwife a democratic and sustainable future, and for a liberated Palestine.

- **Corey Stano** (they/them) is a queer writer and artist living on Florida's Space Coast.

Their work has previously appeared in Impostor: A Poetry Journal and Vita & the Woolf Literary Journal.

❖ **Crystal Rivera** (they/she), is a queer poet and recipe developer from NYC that wants a free Palestine. Born a Russian-Puerto Rican Jew in Queens, NY, many dishes merge cuisines into poems. You can follow them on Instagram @crystal.e.rivera.

❖ **Daniel Schulz** (he/him) is a U.S.-German writer known for various publications in journals such as Gender Forum, the Milton Review, and Fragmented Voices. He has published two chapbooks, Welfare State and No Change to Abuse. IG: @danielschulzpoet

❖ **Danielle Barr** (she/her) is a stay-at-home mom and writer. She was recently named the winner of the Driftwood Press annual short story contest and is querying her first novel. She lives in rural Appalachia with her husband and four young children.

❖ **Derek R. Smith** (he/him) is a public health professional and Anishinaabe two-spirit poet. He has recent publications in Great Lakes Review, San Pedro River Review, ¡Pa'lante!, euphony, Hearth & Coffin, Inlandia, Lucky Jefferson and others.

❖ **Devon Webb** (she/her) is a writer & editor based in New Zealand, with work published extensively worldwide. She is a founding member of The Circus (@circuslit), a collective prioritising radical inclusivity within the indie lit scene.

❖ **Dua'a Almadhoun** is a wife & mother of 4 children who represents all Palestinian women who are struggling all the time to protect and take care of their family under this horrible war. She spreads love and positive energy to face the complicated circumstances they are living every day. She prays for prevailing peace all over the world and she dreams of living the day when Palestine will be free. Free, free Palestine 🍉 🍉

❖ **Elizabeth Day** (she/her) is an author, poet, blogger, and playwright from Las Vegas, Nevada. She is a student at Southern Utah University studying English education and double minors in theater and film. You can find her on Instagram @itsanadventur.

❖ **Eman Alhaj Ali** is a writer, storyteller, and translator from Palestine. She holds a bachelor's degree in English literature and translation with aspirations to continue postgraduate studies. Writing and reading are her passions.

❖ **Emma Loomis-Amrhein** (she/her) is a trans writer and naturalist. Her debut poetry collection, evening primroses, is available from Recenter Press. Her writing has been nominated for BOTN and Pushcart, and lives in over a dozen publications.

❖ **Erika Gill** (they/them) lives, writes and builds community in Denver, CO. Erika is Editor in Chief of Alternative Milk Magazine. Their poetry may be found in Rigorous, Sublunary Review, Birdy, and other spaces. Twitter: @invariablyso

❖ **Ez Naive** is the virtual identity of **Elli Zogia**. Elli is a Greek artist currently living and creating on the traditional, unceded, and ancestral lands of the Coast Salish peoples, including the territories of the Musqueam, Squamish, and Tsleil-Waututh Nations. Through her art, she is exploring themes of motherhood, sexuality, intersectional feminism & magical realism. She is inspired by raw emotion & nature.

- ❖ **Fiona Dignan** (she/her) started writing during lockdown to cope with the chaos of home-schooling four children. She is a Puschcart Prize Nominated poet and writer.

- ❖ **Genevieve Chornenki** (she/her) is an author, editor, poet, and literacy coach with a background in dispute resolution. Her poems have been accepted for publication by the League of Canadian Poets, Friends Quarterly, Prairie Fire, and other print and online publications in Canada, the UK, and Australia. She lives in Toronto, Canada.

- ❖ **Grace R. Reynolds** (she/her) is the author of two poetry collections from Curious Corvid Publishing, Lady of The House (2022) and The Lies We Weave (2023). Connect with her on Instagram @spillinggrace or visit www.spillinggrace.com.

- ❖ **Halley Kunen** is a native-NYC activist. She proudly hosted the Garment Worker Center at her high school. She is also a passionate poet, musician, and performer, and she wants to inspire all to advocate for their mental health, rights, and freedom.

- ❖ **henry 7. reneau, jr.** (he/him/I/me) has work published in Superstition Review, TriQuarterly, Prairie Schooner, Zone 3; Poets Reading the News and Rigorous. His work has also been nominated multiple times for the Pushcart Prize and Best of the Net.

- ❖ **Ifunanya Georgia Ezeano** is an author and poet. She was shortlisted for British Loft Prize for Flash Fiction. She reads, writes and just wants to live.

- ❖ **Jiang Pu** is an educational leader and nature advocate based in the San Francisco Bay Area of California. Her recent poems have appeared in California Quarterly, Caesura, Topical Poetry, among others. www.jiangpu.org

- ❖ **Julia Travers** (she/they) is a writer in Virginia, U.S.A. Find her at Fish Publishing, Rattapallax, On Being, Rough Cut Press, Ecological Citizen, The Poetry Society of Virginia, juliatravers.journoportfolio and on Instagram @jtravers_wordspics.

- ❖ **Julissa Beltran** (she/her) is a Mexican American college student from South Carolina. Her work has been featured in Other Women Worldly Press, Broken Ink, Audience Askew, and Wingless Dreamer Publisher. She strives to be a voice for her community

- ❖ **Leo Rose Rodriguez** is a queer Jewish writer, artist, and activist based in Minneapolis. They are the author of the chapbook Fatherland, Motherland and forthcoming hybrid collection ...and this would be Moshiach: Jewish Writings for Palestine.

- ❖ **Linda M. Crate** (she/her) is a Pennsylvanian writer who has published twelve poetry chapbooks, the latest being: Searching Stained Glass Windows For An Answer (Alien Buddha Publishing, December 2022).

- ❖ **Lyss Stainer** (they/them) is an autistic, trans & anti-zionist Jewish bookseller, writer, and poet. They have been published in Dyke Diaries, In Parentheses, and others. You can find them on Instagram talking about books @librarysoflyss.

- ❖ **Mahnoor Ali** is a flash fiction addict with a fantasyland and she has a bold way of morphing words of her mind into reality of her sentences. She is also currently working on her new project hijr with series of words and also few of her works are published by aspiring pens before. She is a doctor to be, student under Shifa Tameer e Millat University. She can often be found baking up new ways to procrastinate. Literature has always been a sanctuary for the magical galaxy of fantasy and imagination that resides inside her, a realm where her words dance freely like a leaf of willow creating a profound impact on readers. With each key stroke, her emotions become ink and sentences morph into a beautiful tale. She is a lady of action, a sparkling reality ready to light the world with "Noor" of her perspectives

- ❖ **Marcella Cavallo** (she/her) is a German poet with Italian roots. For her, inspiration is found everywhere, as long as you keep your eyes and heart open. Her work appeared in the "Songs of Revolution" Anthology published by Sunday Mornings at the river.

- ❖ **Meredith MacLeod Davidson** is a poet and writer from Virginia, currently based in Scotland. Meredith's poetry is published or forthcoming in The London Magazine, Puerto del Sol, trampset, Cream City Review, Propel Magazine, The Boiler, Gutter, and elsewhere.

- ❖ **Myfanwy Williams** (she/her) is a queer Filipino-Welsh writer, academic and pro-Palestinian activist from Sydney. Her poetry has been published by Between the Fences, Plumwood Mountain Journal, About Place Journal and the Winged Moon Literary Journal.

- ❖ **Nazaret Ranea** (she/her) is an emerging poet recognised as one of Scotland's Next Generation Young Makars. She has published the zines My Men and My Women, and edited the anthology For Those Who Tend the Soil. More info on www.nazaretranea.com

- ❖ **O.P. Jha's** (He/Him) 150 pieces appeared in Rigorous, Mantis, Punt Volat, Discretionary Love, In Parentheses, Shot Glass Journal, Lothlorien Poetry, ANTHRA Zine, The Interwoven Journal, The Cry Lounge, The Odessa Collective, Homer's Odyssey & others.

- ❖ **Peggy May** (she/they) is a Filipino writer from Florida who finds inspiration in everything. In their free time, she likes to daydream and burrow themselves in music. You can find her on Instagram @peggymaypoetry and @peggymayprose.

- ❖ **Prudence Brooks** (she/her) is a disabled poet residing in Portland, Oregon. Prudence has been writing creatively since age nine, and her poems and prose have appeared in Feral Journal of Poetry and Art, Eunoia Review, and Pile Press, among others.

- ❖ **Ramona McCloskey** (she/her) is an archaeologist, multidisciplinary artist and writer from Ireland. Her essays, poetry and short fiction can be found on stonesoilandsoul.substack.com where she writes from a deeply ecocentric and decolonial perspective.

- ❖ **Ranjith Sivaraman** (He/Him) is an upcoming Poet from Kerala, a beautiful state in India. His poems merge nature imagery, human emotions, and human psychology into a gorgeous tapestry of philosophy. https://ranjithsivaraman.com

- ❖ **Ri Ekl,** mathematician, amateur physicist and artist born in Budapest as the only son of academic parents on April 4, 1984. He writes and composes poems and music.

- ❖ **Roberta Gould's** work has appeared widely in mags, blogs, anthologies including. The

Art and Craft of Poetry, editor Daisy Aldan, Mixed Voices, A Slant of Light, Mid Amerian Review, Green Mountain, Confrontation, Crescendo, Home Planlet News, Socialism and Democracy, Ikon. Her books include Day True, (Mountain Lion Publishing) Talk When You Can(Presa). Woven Lightning. (Spuyten Duyvil) In Houses With Ladders, Waterside Press, Esta Naranja and a forthcoming Kindle, also in Spanish. Atravesar Web sites robertagould.net robertagould.substack.com

- **Saige England** is based in Aotearoa, New Zealand. Author of The Seasonwife, her best-selling debut novel, she has a background as an award-winning journalist reporting from conflict zones, and she is an award-winning poet. Savannah Jade (she/her) is a queer, multiracial writer from CA and a current MFA candidate at Emerson College. She published a volume of poetry, Began with a Rose, at the age of 17, and her other writings have appeared in Moss Puppy Magazine and Page Turner Magazine. For more, visit her website: www.jadepoetry.com

- **Salem Paige** (they/them) is a queer, transgender poet whose works revolve around the exploration of identity and discomfort through the spaces where Nature and technology intertwine. Their first collection, The Third Self, was published in 2023.

- **Sara Santistevan** (she/her/ella) is an emerging Latina poet. In both her artistic and editorial work, Sara aims to build bridges between historical and personal narratives and amplify diverse voices in literature.

- **Savannah Jade** (she/her) is a queer, multiracial writer from CA and a current MFA candidate at Emerson College. She published a volume of poetry, Began with a Rose, at the age of 17, and her other writings have appeared in Moss Puppy Magazine and Page Turner Magazine. For more, visit her website: www.jadepoetry.com.

- A poet out of Durham, NC, **Sebastian Ellios** (he/him) writes about what it means to partake in human ecosystems. He's published by Tabadul Collective, Voicemail Poems, Fruitslice, & Carolina Muse. Find him on IG @sebastianellios or at sebastianellios.com

- **Shahryar Eskandari Zanjani** is a writer, teacher, and editor. His poetry has received an honorable mention in the 2024 Witness Poetry Prize competition (Southern Humanities Review 57.3), won second place in Nine Muses Review's inaugural poetry contest, and appeared in The Hemlock Anthology (Lighted Lake Press, 2024). Shahryar's debut book, English Phonetics and Phonology for Farsiphones, was published by Booka (2020). He has edited several books at ATU Press and is the translator of Zahhak's Inferno (Markosia, 2024). His work has also appeared in Willow Review, Sky Island Journal, and Thimble, among others. Shahryar lives in Tehran, Iran.

- A South Carolina Arts Commission fellowship recipient, **Terri McCord** has earned awards from Hub City, Emrys Foundation, Southeast Review, and Vermont Studio Center. Her poems have been nominated for "Best of the Net" and four Pushcarts.

- **Tor Purrett** works as an animist artist creating textile pieces through ritual which hold an intention. She works with the crafts of spinning, natural dying and weaving, creating everything from natural materials using her spinning wheel, dye pot and loom.

- **Yoda Olinyk** (she/they) is a writer, editor, and workshop guide from Canada. Her work has appeared in many beloved journals and she has two books out. You can find her at www.doulaofwords.com

❖ **Yuna Kang** is a queer, Korean-American writer based in Northern California. They were nominated for the 2022 Dwarf Stars Award, as well as the 2024 Best New Poets Award. Their website link is: https://kangyunak.wixsite.com/website

❖ **Zehnab Hayat** is a 21-year-old writer based in England. Her work explores the delicate balance between the beauty and tragedies of humanity, often highlighting the intertwining nature of both. With a strong focus on the Palestinian cause, Zehnab's narratives challenge perspectives and delve into the grey areas of life, aiming to engage and provoke thought. Writing for her is not just a profession, but a powerful tool to reshape how audiences see the world.

❖ **Zeid** (he/they) is an author, poet, and scientist from Jordan. They've been writing poetry for almost a decade, and are thrilled to appear in *We Were Seeds* by *Querencia Press.*

❖ **Zianna Ruiha** (she/they) (Ngāti Toa) is a queer, disabled creative procrastinator from Aotearoa. She believes in the liberation of all indigenous peoples in the world, and the power of art in reflecting and hoping for this.